DEATH

is my

SHEPHERD

David Castleman's

DEATH

is my

SHEPHERD

ArtWord . White Bear Lake . Minnesota . 2002

Published in the United States of America by
ArtWord
5273 Portland Avenue
White Bear Lake, MN 55110 USA

Cover design and photos by David Castleman
Printed by Bang Printing, Brainerd, MN

This is a work of fiction. Any resemblance to actual events or persons, living or dead, is entirely coincidental.

Library of Congress Control Number: 2002103811

ISBN 0-9678104-2-6

Contents

Gimmy and my mother and I never pretended too successfully that we were much of what is commonly called a family, but occasionally he or she would toss out an effort and for a brief while he or she would almost pretend that we were a loving bunch, and approximately respectable. I do remember when some famous local resident died in an unsavory fashion and most of the citizenry was in mourning publicly, with flags caught halfway up the poles, and Gimmy's and my mother's customers wept and exclaimed about how such things shouldn't ought to happen in a dignified community.

The local preacher passed the word that he was going to throw a special memorial shindig, and Gimmy and my mother fooled themselves once again by pretending that even such trash as they were included in the invitation. But of course a whore and a barkeep couldn't realistically expect their customers to recognize them while in church, or to want to be reminded that the church wasn't the only playground in town.

We dressed up fit to kill, almost like Astaire and Ginger Rogers but with a calmlier spiffiness, and like a family of ducks we marched along the street and to the church along with all of our customers and everybody. Everybody avoided us a bit, I noticed, leaving a ring of space around us like an aura or an extended halo, or like an expulsion of bad breath.

Even in the church everybody avoided us, especially folks we'd been joking with just hours before. Eyes that had exchanged individual informations with us just hours earlier, were now the eyes of absolute strangers.

Perhaps that's because everybody was so busy crying, especially if they felt they were being observed. Especially among the ladies, nobody was about to be outdone in their display of mourning. Even my mother did her best to be one of the girls, wailing and sniffling, and I do believe that Gimmy might have shed a tear or two except that he had probably forgotten how to cry, it being so long since he had had any feelings.

I had never learned how to cry, so it wouldn't have done me much good to try, and I didn't bother. I knew people were watching me surreptitiously, that they snuck peeks between their fingers, and such, but because I didn't know what could be done about it I didn't bother to do anything at all. I just sat there feeling kind of stupid.

Eventually the death march leaked out from somewhere in the sacred depths of mystery, somewhere up behind the podium, I thought, and the preacher was through with his preaching, and he preceded everybody else out of the church. He opened the big front doors and he stood on the porch to shake hands and to let everybody know he had seen them and would mention it in the proper quarters, and he smiled big as Santa.

And yet somehow as Gimmy and my mother and I were approaching him he swung his broad backside

toward us and somehow he just didn't quite see us.
Events conspired against us, once again, and we moved in
that little circle of absence. We were, therefore, the only
folks he missed shaking hands with, so I guessed he'd be
unable to tell Santa's boss we'd been there. I was
pondering that.

As if a moment had been yanked conspicuously out
of time, everybody's attention appeared to be elsewhere
and his eye caught my eye, and he winked at me.
Nobody was on the earth except for him and me, just for
that moment, and he winked at me, one evil wink.

His sentience leaped out through that shuttering eye
and exploded instantly in my consciousness, and with
one forefinger's tip he plugged his nostril and he blew
sharply, and he launched a snotrocket that crashed
exactly on the tip of my forward shoe. And once again
he winked at me, the evillest wink I ever did see.

Always it is our anticipation that every priest and
preacher is a pompous windbag and a pedophile,
pulpitting paeans to his phantom foreskin and to the
conscientious depravity of the soul he has not, and we'd
be surprised if ever we discovered an exception, and that
exception would probably starve, I suppose, knowing us.

Similarly, my parents were as bad almost as it was
convenient for them to be. They were like preachers,
lawyers for the cosmic meaninglessness, honorless as
bugs.

His aim was such a winner I supposed he must have
had quite a bit of practice, and I pictured him alone in
his vestry with his feet on the desk and a single malt
scotch in his hand, as with his other hand he fired
salvoes into the wastebasket, into the face of the clock,
at the photograph that smiled openly on his desk.

I knew what he drank because he had a private room

upstairs in Gimmy's saloon, and sometimes in daytime I had cleaned the messes he had left there, using much very hot soapy water. And I had made deliveries after dark to the back door of the vestry, whose entry was concealed between two very steep hedges, and whose lights were invisible to the peasantry, as he was fond of calling his customers.

Always as I had approached either of those rooms, located along either of those dark private corridors, I had heard crying sounds from within the room, and not all of the crying had been his, I suspected. When I had knocked a shuffled mumbling had been heard within, and a scraping sound, and maybe a thump or two. I figured he kept babies in a sack.

If I was startled, discouraged, or disappointed by his performance, it was not to discover his hypocrisy, since hypocrisy is to be expected among the clergy. Every preacher has a small man's complex, and a woman who has a small man's complex is the worst.

If I was surprised, it was only because he was so good in his deceptions. I can appreciate talent, and genius drops my jaw. I doubt he was a genius, but he was damned good.

Personally, I'm a lousy liar. I tried it a bunch of times, but just can't get the hang of it. He got the hang of it just fine. He was an artiste of the first water in the art of lying.

"Come on, Working Boy. You ain't dead yet," was my most commonly heard mantra. It was never a summons I used myself, but it was commonly a summons which was used toward me by my controllers as if they were rather cruelly imploring the listening eye of the cosmos. Whenever they suspected me of experiencing a reverie they would summon me with such harsh words, and instantly I would be snatched back from whatever peacefulness I dawdled in.

I am not Cellini, and what follows is no autobiography complete with surgical nips and tucks designed to create an existence I would prefer. I am not a clever fellow, certainly not clever enough to parade before your mind fictitious circumstances. And such a monumentally unclever character as I am can hide behind few obstructions quite so completely as he can hide behind the truth.

My goal is to portray my friend Grit, my benefactor, my freshly claimed father, my personal savior. He concocted this thing I am, like some hoary ancient alchemist using bits of this and pieces of that, gathered distantly when the moon eclipsed or when the sun. What gratitude I possess I fling around him like a great comfortable coat, and possess it still. Of his aura of beneficence I partake however minimally.

He was a poet, and his mind processed his wordings while he was awake and while he slept. His was genius, and he was mostly ignored while he lived, because he was misunderstood and because he was understood too well by those who should have known better.

I am not certain he had much of any individual personality, and am fairly certain he had almost no discernible ego. He was as if a light had streamed in from some celestial elsewhere, illumining.

I would almost prefer a perfect reticence, to hold quite still about the man, but his reflection does not permit me such indulgence: his finger wags at cowardice, at selfishness, and I must comply. He continues to inhabit me, and he talks to me there, though I know it is not he.

Once upon a time I asked him why, of all the misbegotten wanderlings available to him, he selected me for his patronage. He replied, more cryptically perhaps than archly, that it was unwise to ask a question if one did not actually wish to receive its answer. "Innocence is bliss, one of the finest blisses of all," he commented.

"You were the ugliest animal of all my eyes had glanced upon. You were heroically ill-used, bloody at head and bottom, and your mind hadn't yet created itself from the essential chaos," he said.

"And a whore is not the best of mothers, and a barkeep is not the best of fathers, at any time. And everybody needs a living friend sometimes, or he will build friends in his mind to his destruction," he said.

It was not my job to resent his statements. As corollary to his absence of ego, he was also curiously absent of any actual malice, as far as I was able to tell, and I freely confess that I did look exceedingly carefully. Such an absence appeared to me to be uncannily inhuman, placing this man among some other species, almost, though I do suppose there might have been others who were similarly afflicted.

Grit was for awhile fond of frequenting the saloon I was a runner for, which the man I considered to be effectually my father owned, he said, and where he was the prominent barkeep. My father's name was Gimmy, with a hard g, though I suppose some few folks might have spelled it Gimmee, attributing his name to his grasping nature.

I remember being told that Gimmy was an abbreviation for Gimlet, and that this sobriquet had been dealt him because some penally inclined wags had decided that his eyes resembled 2 gin martinis up, with onions rolling slowly and untetheredly around on the bottom of each glass. His eyes did appear to act with no synchronicity, which was unnerving.

Grit always ordered a single imperial pint of India Pale Ale, which was the only good beer sold in Gimmy's saloon, THE NIGHTLY STUMBLE. Mostly what Gimmy's menu sported was the common junk, dead beer in cans, which the proletariats do so love, so to speak.

Even now, all of these long round years later, I believe I can remember seeing Grit when he would come in for his beer. He never engaged in the fools' hilarity of booze, with those other patrons who shouted and laughed and watched the sports contests on the television, cheering for heroes through whom they lived vicariously. He wasn't remarkably gloomy in appearance, either, but just sat within himself, sometimes looking but more often not bothering to look.

Early in his visits to the saloon, my mother invited him upstairs to one of those rooms she entertained her customers in, but he declined her hospitalities and she soon desisted her offers. She could see he wanted only the companionship of beer, memory, and his dreams.

I heard Gimmy say to her, "Dorothy, you're not in Kansas anymore. Leave the man alone. Breaching broads ain't that one's schtick," and she responded by just walking away, not bothering to sulk, just treating it as business. Mother was a reasonable whore.

Her name wasn't Dorothy.

Except for my mother that time or two accosting him as he sat insured in silence, Grit was never bothered by anyone. The screaming yahoos ignored him, being at heart responsible people, and seeing his carriage and seeing those more superficial aspects of his character. His face was commonly frozen in its features as if he had suffered a stroke, and his gaze elsewhere, nowhere, or unidentifiable. But sometimes his face was quite animated, or at least sometimes his eyes were animated, and sometimes his lips twitched as if he were speaking, or as if he were, as I discovered later, assembling, disassembling, and reassembling sentences.

His hair atop was longish or shortish, depending upon the accident of the seasons, and always he had something of a beard, fully covering, sometimes longish and sometimes shortish. He had arms like Abraham Lincoln's arms were described in Charnwood's or in Sandburg's stories, revealing, perhaps, a muscularly demanding youth, and his chest was a barrel organ that produced a symphonic speaking voice. His voice was big and round, modulated, sometimes deep and resonantly melodious and sometimes a strangled bass.

He had, I noticed, almost no eyebrows, his generally nordic coloring muting their appearance almost to invisibility. His ears, like Montaigne's, were small and flat. Sometimes his face twitched, or shuddered, also betraying some previous stroke, I thought.

All of this fit ill, I later thought, with his frequently rather impish sense of humor. Another man's humor can be difficult to appreciate especially if our own mind lacks elasticity, I discovered frequently, too frequently.

Sometimes when business was slow and my services as a runner, or saloon's delivery boy, were uncalled for, I would sit in the shadows at the top of the stairs in the saloon, and I'd watch Gimmy doing his sisyphean labors for the clientele, and I'd watch my mother ditto performing those portions of her tasks which might be viewed. Grit caught me at my watching once and, when next he saw me traipsing the saloon floor, he asked me what occurred in my mind as I watched those same old goings on day after day and night after night of my young life.

I replied, after watching him during the space of a pause, that I studied rats in a cage unconscious of their captivity. His half-invisible eyebrows shot up, changing aspects of their relative invisibility as their shadows moved when the lights angled against them differently.

He asked me to join him, and he gestured toward a chair. I hesitated, glancing toward Gimmy, toward my mother, fearing disapproval which was defensive and inevitable. I sat, and Gimmy's thousand yard stare was sucked into a focus upon me and he said, "Mister, leave the kid alone. He's got work to do."

Grit gestured to me to stay, and he stood and walked to the bartable or counter, just where Gimmy stood on the other side with his shoulders hunched up and both palms flat on the counter, a wet rag trailing out from under the palm of his sinister hand. Grit smiled as disarmingly as was convenient or available to him, and upon the counter he rang one of those old peace-type silver dollars.

"I'm a sports reporter, and I just want to know what the kid thinks about the chances of our getting into the play-offs this year. The public has a right to know what the future thinks about sports, which are after all is said and done the most important thing in a man's life, I think. What do you think?" Grit said to the man.

Gimmy responded with a sullenly condescending sneer, said, "It's your money and your time on the meter, friend," and continued to wipe the greasy counter with his greasy rag. Grit returned to me, just as he was always to return to me, and he sat and sipped his beer leaving a thin moustache of foam overlaying his thicker moustache of fur.

His lip spoke to his tongue and his tongue snuck out and grappled, and the lesser moustache was gone. Like the snows of yesteryear, I did not yet think, though that would come in its allotted time.

"Do you know the fable of the pied piper of Hamelin? He too had rats to deal with, and he dealt well as a dealer must," Grit began.

"Many years ago on the european subcontinent a very nasty man was very mean and nasty to people he could be mean and nasty to. His name was Larry and like Shakespeare's nasty brothers in TITUS ANDRONICUS he raped a young girl and he dis-handed her," Grit said, watching the widening eyes that watched him across the table.

"He was so mean that folks had shunned him for years, till he was forced to live in a tent on the edge of a lake, a little tent with a little portable potty on a wee hillock inches or feet away from the waters. The sheriff could not touch him because in an attempt to be fair to folks who had been abused the laws had become enfeebled, though everybody knew what he had done.

"But the brothers of the young girl watched him steadily from a great and a legal distance. One of the brothers was an excellent hunter, with magnificent predatorial eyes, and he trapped a hundred rats, big furry ones with big hungry tummies and with sharp claws and needle-pointed teeth.

"Larry came to town for his provisions, just as he always came to town for his provisions, and he stopped off in the saloon on his way back, just as he always stopped off in the saloon on his way back. While he was using the washroom, where of course he did not actually wash anything, one of the brothers finagled into his glass a drop of an intense equatorial laxative, and the brother returned dutifully to the lakeside. Larry returned to his drink, wiping his fingers on the front of his trousers, wiping idly and without disgust.

"Meanwhile the other brother, the brother who was an excellent hunter, filled the portable potty's reservoir with his hundred rats in a sack. The brothers talked almost not at all. They had done with talking on this matter, and the time was come for action.

"The sound of the returning pickup truck told the brothers it was time to hide, and so they did hide in the trees. Larry returned with his provisions and he began to unload the provisions into his tent. Somewhat suddenly he stood upright, erect as the mind should be, as he felt a tickling in his bowels.

"He walked, a bit more rapidly than was customary for him, to the potty and he opened the door and he went in, and as he went in the brothers ran close and slipped through the doorhasp a twist of hempen rope, and about the potty they tied a length of hempen rope, securing the door. Larry yelled, and the potty was pushed gently and swiftly onto its back, and like a canoe it was pushed onto the small waves of the lake.

"Larry yelled, and Larry was yelling, and it was only a matter of moments before he disturbed the sack, whose knot had been contrived to achieve an exact behavior. For almost an hour, or perhaps an hour or two, Larry could be heard screaming in his slowly sinking canoe.

"Many people around the lake heard Larry's screams, but nobody tried to help him. It was not the yellings, nor perhaps the screams, that made the eeriest noise, but it was those several yelpings," Grit said, and as he watched me I thought I could discern in his eyes a movement as if a shark were turning underwater a few feet beyond my accurate vision, and then it resembled the dancing of a leprechaun in a shaded glen just too far away.

"What lives in that man's mind," I wondered, placidly.

"The meter's up," said Gimmy. "Working Boy, shuffle them things."

A companionable opponent.

Once a week or so, after this curious beginning, Grit would come into the barroom and give Gimmy an extra dollar if I chanced to be there also, and he and I would sit at some peripheral table and he would discourse or we would chat, or he would ask me questions. It was for me a new fun, a hospitable entertainment. It was fun to be used for something so very noncapitalistic, so undemeaning.

Mostly my job consisted of delivering booze, cigarettes, sandwiches, lottery tickets, and such, to neighbors of the saloon, from morning until the closing in the night when morning was almost apparent once again. Some customers wanted me to visit with them those rooms my mother kept upstairs, and my mother would have approved, but Gimmy always said no. "If the truck carries too heavy a load, pretty soon you don't have no truck no more, and that's that." Some few occasions she'd whine about her needing the help, but whining wheedled nothing out of Gimmy, and he was obdurate.

And so on went the closing of our years.

Sometimes I was called to deliver various items to Grit, or rather Mr. Grit as I called him in those days, and typically these items might be such things as a tin of sardines or tuna, a large live ale, a specifically named type of bread that was sold in one local store only, soy sprouts or an onion. He told me that his days of tobacco, of hard booze, of lottery tickets, were long by the wayside, long dead.

Sometimes as a tip he gave me another of those old silver dollars, morgan or peace, and oftentimes that thing exactly was used as a bribe to allow Gimmy to send me to him, or to sit with him in the saloon.

And whenever I delivered to him in his apartment he fed me with just whatever he was eating also. I think Gimmy suspected this duplicity but forgave me because he considered it a financial boon for himself, which I suppose it was. At meals in the saloon I seldom asked for more.

I had seldom tasted fresh fruits and fresh vegetables before, and I confess that I grew fond of them. Perhaps I had thought that fruits and vegetables were grown in cans, much as some fruits are placed in bottles when the fruits are merely blossoms, and so they grow almost to maturity in those bottles which are later removed and filled the rest of the way with liqueurs or with fancy oils.

Grit and I slowly became accustomed to one another, and familiarity bred contentment. And so eventually I became his chattel, not simply his pupil but his slave.

It was once upon a time in the early afternoon when Grit arrived at my all-hope-abandoned home, THE NIGHTLY STUMBLE, and he walked deliberately to the greasy bar where with a greasy rag Gimmy polished the greasy counter using dull unembarrassed movements. The two men talked just a smidgin below the level of my hearing and then Grit lifted to the counter a purple velvet bag with golden drawstrings. The bag contained a hundred silver dollars, the real ones.

Gimmy's fat rag tongued the bag from the greasy counter.

Gimmy said, "Where did you get them things anyhow," and Gimmy was not a man to ask questions until he didn't need to know.

Grit responded, "They were a manna of my patrimony, and being manna they never really belonged to me," and as he turned his back to Gimmy it was evident that to his consciousness Gimmy had just disappeared, been swallowed by the fungi of the earth, or eaten by the black eels of the sea, or sucked off to the stars.

Gimmy nodded to me, where I had been shoving a broom, and he said, "Come on, Working Boy. You ain't dead yet," and he laughed in a consumptive gurgle, like a drain yanking mud through the floor. "Working Boy, you don't want no more of me, I thinks."

As Grit eyed at me I followed in his wake toward and through the saloon's doors. They didn't bother to swing much when I went through. I needed to sleep for a year, until the dark spell was past.

Mother was a wraith, an undeveloped image on a plate, a photograph left too long in the sunlight upon a windowsill, the memory of an image as the image passes across the horizons of the mind forever, something like that or like one of those, I suppose. Gimmy was more substantial in his way, because he could never understand that an ability to compromise might be a desirable ability or might be an ability to pursue, and he never could understand that happiness was a worthy goal: he revelled in the potential triumph of his individual selfishness, though he revelled grovellingly.

As we passed toward and then through the vertical plane of the doorway neither Grit nor I looked back at his predecessors to my existence. They passed into some other plane of consciousness as we passed through that very identifiable plane of the purely physical. They became literally despicable, things unworthy of an active consideration, almost.

Grit and I did not walk jauntily, nor did we stride like proud men stride on a deliberate mission, but we walked as blandly and as realistically as ever did the evil midges of capitalism walk on their appointed rounds of depredation, of business. Our spirits were tucked away until the time approved.

Since I had never had a mother or a father for any certainty, but had been spun into existence by some broken-fingered weavers in a purgatorial threads-mill, I was uncertain wholly. My fingers and my toenails had always trailed among ethereal waters of eternity, and I had therefore been a meat for the surface-dwellers.

Unarticulated suspicions performed throughout my psyche like a distant spectacle of lights. It was exhilarating to suspect that I wasn't ever to be beaten again, that much of my past was passed.

Being beaten is ungood, I thought though not in words. Being beaten suspends the psyche in blue flame and the psyche burns withinwards, always shimmering toward dissolution.

Gimmy, in his cups or sober, would thrash me for his pleasure. Later I would wake dazed and bloodied on the rug or on the cold boards of the floor. My mouth and my nose had run with blood, of course, and my ears and my anus. Often I wondered fleetingly why no blood had run from my eyes, from my nails, from nipples, from navel. I wondered why no blood had come from my penis, from the tender insides of my elbows and knees, from armpits, from the soft pit where the legs meet. And that was why I carried everywhere the animal that lived inside my ears. What it did I did not know. But I did know how it had been put there, and that it stayed there restlessly, always. And every sometime in awhile it shifted its position: it moved, like a monstrous bird in a tiny church, a bird bigger almost than the church.

As the light of external consciousness penetrated my psyche naturally I became superficial and exocentric, and my wonder ceased concerning self. Focus wandered elsewhere, where a world exists. I was grateful for the existence of an external world, a world that was not I.

Being wise for a child, perhaps, I held my exhilaration close, lest it be taken from me, and had I felt I might have felt that not even our tortured genius of Nazareth might have discerned it had his eyes held mine. Carefully I was.

Grit and I walked several blocks back to his apartment, a modest arrangement of rooms tucked in the upper story of a large building whose streetlevel was a warren of mostly tiny shops purveying superficial extraneous items to superficial extraneous people who chanced to have too much cash or too much credit. His personal entrance was around in the rear of the building beside his dilapidated garage which contained his obviously world-weary toyota pickup truck held together by almost a mile of ducttape.

He stored unnecessary possessions in big black garbage bags, in the back of the truck and casually placed in the garage. He claimed that nobody would bother a big black garbage bag carelessly secured, especially if it were guarded by a truck as disreputable-looking as was his.

The lengths of ducttape periodically would peel from the truck, and water would run in from the rains and in early spring frequently he had a crop of mushrooms growing inside the truck. When he got around to it, he would reapply the tape amid an internal fanfare cheering his sense of industriousness.

I had brought deliveries to his apartment many times but I had never quite bothered to focus upon the place. On this occasion I was duly impressed by his available solitude, although the rooms were stuffed like a glutton's belly.

Grit ignored me while I wandered entrancedly, understanding, I suppose, my reaction. I had been a captive in a little space and was now to be a captive in a big space, and so I anticipated an uncoiling. He had a thousand books and a thousand vinyl records and a thousand videos.

He told me that many of the videos were illegal bootlegs of music, compilations he had spliced chronologically, of individual performances. He liked one tape to feature one single performer, so he could study the personality and its idiosyncrasies. Typically he watched these performances during those evenings he sipped his jammy red wines.

His favorites varied as the months rode by, and his favorite of the moment was something called CAROLS FROM ATLANTA: THE 70TH ANNIVERSARY MOREHOUSE-SPELMAN CHRISTMAS CAROL CONCERT. He called it his forgiveness album, he said. He said that one of the women choristers had a face and a smile like a church's stained glass window through which an angel watched in smiling beneficence.

Attempting to appear to be doing something quite otherwise, I pondered that rather seventeenth-century remark, and I sought to understand it. Temporizing, and to elicit more and pertinent information, I asked him what other videos displayed for him the spectrum of the sacred, what others he deemed special in his approach toward some measure of contentment.

He said he had collated almost a hundred hours of bootleg videos of the early Bob Dylan on the concert platform, in the most intimately revealing and in the most distant venues. "This was when," Grit commented with a wry banality, "the man's genius was so indefinably expansive his brains were hanging out through his ears."

Grit had expended his best and his most duplicitous methodology in acquiring every specific available video recording of Billie Holiday's phenomenal performances, and with indefatigable pains he spliced them together sequentially according to exact chronology. And so the whole, which was a matter of almost four hours, appeared almost to be a single lengthy uninterrupted concert.

And he did similarly with Louis Armstrong and with Rosemary Clooney, with Sarah Vaughan, each at their peaks. And he did similarly with Hank Williams. Body language can be everything in music, almost, when we are sufficiently privileged to witness it. Because music approaches a spiritual athletics, displaying a virtual pathway that is not itself.

He paused, and something in his mind ticked, and he understood my curious predicament. He glanced directly into my interior mechanism, and he said, "Yes. It is an indulgence, that we insist in accusing our deity of consciousness. One of our appetites condemns us for such bravado, realizing that all bravado is childish, and a profounder appetite forgives us.

"This difference is demonstrated clearly when we experience choral singing, and we witness as it vacillates between submission and joy," he said. As he was talking he was walking toward the television, and then he played that video he mentioned, CAROLS FROM ATLANTA. He asked that I sit, shut my mind, and absorb.

I did, and I believe he did. It was a rarity.

Finally the spectacle of singing was passed, and I was returned from whatever special charity of being I had experienced. Grit remained beside me, and I was glad that, though we had been apart, we had somehow been together. It was enough.

He withdrew the cassette, and he set it beside him on a small table, and he said, "We are going to be friends, and friendship requires a few exceedingly vital rules." He steepled his hands as he bent forward and he craned his elbows just up from his knees.

He spoke softly, in his deep soft insistent melody. "Honor thy fellow creatures and thou dost honor thyself. Honor thyself and thou dost honor thy fellow creatures. Therefore: honor thyself, and honor thy fellows, and blessings be upon every thing.

"Thou shalt never harm a fellow creature's body, nor shalt thou harm that fellow's feelings, (which is the same,) especially in jest.

"Thy body shall be clean as thy circumstances permit, clean as thou canst reasonably contrive, and thy mind also. Laugh cleanly, and laugh abundantly, for laughter represents forgiveness from the earth.

"Eat green, and be clean."

With a curious formality, he stood and we shook hands. He smiled more broadly than I had ever seen a person smile, more innocently and more knowingly, simultaneously, the way one's mother might smile in her final goodbye. Such a generous smile might blast one's mind.

I smiled also, but my smile was o so smaller, alas.

Grit and I calmly puttered about for awhile, munching sardine sandwiches on a whole-grain wheat-rye bread, with tofu mayo, sprouts and greens of broccoli, and with a merest dollop of marinero sauce. He was doing whatever it was he did, and I was glancing through his libraries, his books and music.

Among his books I might later have been surprised to discover at the least a foot of books by WW Jacobs, almost as much by Tom Aldrich, much of Matt Shiel, (including a first edition of THE PURPLE CLOUD, and a wee handful of well-worn paperbacks of the same book,) BLACK LIGHT by Ron Shaw. And he had a first edition of Ginsberg's weenily acclaimed HOWL, he said, because it made him laugh.

He was a crotchetty misaligned anomaly of a personality, I thought, and his aberrancies could make you roar with anger, or purr with a soft inner glow.

In our postliterate, psychoclastic, cyberplastic society, everything about the man appeared anomalous, I thought. He appeared almost to exude a sweetness deeper than himself although its fumes might be poisonous.

Grit's call intruded into my dazy speculations, "It is movie time, Prometheus." My name was not Prometheus, I knew, and so at first I thought he might be calling his cat whose name I did not yet know was god. The cat had been performing the immemorially ancient cat-dance, the kitticat minuet, by which they try to trip up the feet of whatever human they chance to be near, by weaving in and out among the human feet.

Grit explained that the lion's share of the loft, (actually he called it the moiety,) was established as a movie theater, and that his guests were expected to arrive soon for an evening of civilized entertainment. Of course I had already known that a theater was in residence on this capacious upper story we shared with a few other tenants, having seen below on the street-level the swinging sign proclaiming THE FINDERS' CLUB.

So discreetly arranged on a swinging disk, only very distantly might the name be considered to be the practicably philosophical equivalent to a stage direction, and an exhortation of sorts.

Grit called THE FINDERS' CLUB a club of gentilesse, saying it was most assuredly not a gentlemen's club. He informed me, once again, that men without women were beasts, and duly lamented that only a very few women chose to come to the club.

Videos were played on a very large screen like a television screen but with an extraordinarily superior definition to any that might be obtained commercially. His screen, as he permitted himself to call it, had been supplied by a technical genius who worked for a zillionaire and who was given excellent perquisites.

In an adjacent room lush breathing ales were supplied gratis to the guests, who expertly though apparently inadvertently deposited generous monetary gestures into individually marked receptacles as they departed each evening.

Mostly, movies were shown on Wednesdays and on Saturdays, although other arrangements could sometimes be made. Mostly, the movies were the common coinage of our minds such as might appeal to any calmly intelligent person, movies such as STAGECOACH, THE THIRD MAN, or a concert by Alan Jay

Lerner. Tonight was the holy grail of music, a 53 minute concert in an intimate setting by Robert Johnson, only very recently discovered and painstakingly unclouded.

Upon asking Grit, I learned that the previous showing had been the James Bond movie ON HER MAJESTY'S SECRET SERVICE, starring George Lazenby as Sean Connery, and also starring the woman who in THE AVENGERS had permanently scarred the psyches of so many adolescent boys, Diana Rigg. Most of the movie patrons were men who remembered her clearly, men who as boys spent many long hours alone with her as their personal sultry siren.

Grit said it was important that people did not revisit their childhoods too frequently, and it was important that they did revisit those places once in a while.

We walked through the hallways and we opened and we closed a few doors, adjusting the locks in anticipation of the coming flow. Soon we were in the preliminary saloon, cafe, or what-you-may-call-it, and the customers eked in.

Some of the people preferred to be greeted shyly, or slyly, or loudly, and Grit could spot each type instantly. Mostly I studied his personal understandings, rather than studying the individuals he greeted.

Many of the men wore what we call baseball caps, which they doffed and set upon their tabletops conspicuously, as if marking their territories, like wolves peeing on the stones and trees.

One spectacle I was bound to witness on several occasions. At one table sat a small clique of chinese fellows alongside of one youngish honkie male, they and he clearly comprising 2 separate groups. He had a baggie containing hardboiled eggs which he ate one by one carefully amid the conversations. Each time he encountered an individual egg the attentions of his companions fascinated upon his procedure. One and by one he held each inviolate eggshell in his left fingers and with his right forefinger's knuckle he rapped the shell at its longitudinal equator causing a surgical point of breakage, and he spun the egg deftly in both hands exactly and caressingly revolving the egg until that exact point was chased into a single line circumscribing the whole shell, that line becoming a fallen circle. Then his fingertips removed 2 perfect crowns and he laid them on his plate like a conqueror, a conqueror of eggs.

The meat was his, and the game went on.

When I did begin to study these people who were so new to my life, I wondered why so many apparently intelligent people wore anything so demonstrably silly as baseball caps. Grit said, "Caps protect the noggin which is precious, and," and here he paused as if for me to mark his words, "if they sport a silly popular slogan they render the wearer almost invisible. Few adults continue to look after they have reached an intelligent maturity, and fewer of those adults bother to inspect anything that brags in such a manner of its rampant imbecility.

"Therefore, the wearing of such motley renders the wearer almost invisible," he continued.

Preaching can be an easy display of apparent virtue, I reflected, because even though Grit pontificated upon the topic in this manner, I did nevertheless notice that his quest for an absolute anonymity was not wholly a genuine quest. He too wore the omnipresent baseball-type cap, but his cap typically sported the logo of some macho lumberyard or timbermill, or of a golf course, a realization which informed me that his pride must be served as competently as must his opinions.

He was a philosopher in search of truth, but he

wanted a comfortable truth. Even Diogenes, I reasoned, probably lied to himself when he was cached in his keg. It's a humane failing.

It is curious to ponder that when the gods peer toward us and through us from their vital distance of omniscience we may be said to exist always in the past tense because their comprehension is complete, and because our language is deficient when used by creatures who inhabit such limitations as we inhabit. Those allegedly omniscient beings must realize that we prey upon ourselves, and that our prayers mouthed the prey as they were spoken, and as our bloody nerves pondered.

I strolled among the tables, observing everything, after he had disappeared into the projector's cockpit to arrange the movie. I observed the people, noticing that every race was ably represented. People sat apart, and people sat in smallish clusters chatting vigorously and amiably of whatever they considered to be entertaining among the myriad literatures of creative expression. Because religion is commonly subsidiary to the politics of race, religion and politics and race were discussed equably. They were eaten raw, without salt.

I observed that on every table, and on every sideboard, was a brief stack of postcards, free for the stealing. One could only surmise the tone in which they had been written.

One card read,   TOBACCO BE TABOO.

One card read,   THE POPE
                  IS MY PILATE,   and this postcard was decorated with a small woodcut of a semitic face peering through a barbedwire fence. The face was a haunting face, and was so exceptionally haggard it

appeared to be hanging from its skull like a casually tossed blanket hangs from a chair.

One card said,   SELF-REFERENTIAL OBSESSION
                     CONQUERS THE WRAITHS OF
                     WISDOM.

One card showed a cartoon of one thick cajun lumberjack warning a tall lumberjack,

                     I HALF YOUR HIGH
                     AND TWICE YOUR WIDE,
                     AND I PASS ON YOUR ASS
                     FOR A PLAY NO,

and the song was a profound guttural growl.

One card said,   LIFT YOUR NIGHTIE.

One card read,   MERCY?
                     DO YOU ASK FOR MERCY?

                     YOU WILL BE GIVEN A TOAD AND
                     A BUCKET OF SALT AND NOTHING
                     MORE.

                     DO NOT ASK FOR MORE.
                     THERE IS NONE.

Cards had been placed discreetly even upon the walls, in some few places. Of course I assumed that my friend Grit was the culprit scribbler, and I wondered if his toes twitched under his writingtable as he had penned these various lines. Clearly he was a seditious inciter.

One card said,	THE BLOODY SOUL OF GERMANY IS GENOCIDE. GERMANY IS FOUNDED ON A BEDEVILMENT BY GENOCIDE.
One card read,	THE JOY OF THE LIVING IS A FEAST FOR THE DEAD.
One card said,	FOR EACH, ONE'S NEIGHBOR IS THE LESSER MARTYR, VAGUELY PRELIMINARY AS WAS CHRIST,
	AND EACH ONE IS JUDAS, BORN TO BARTER SUBSTANCE TOO REAL FOR A SUBSTANCE OF MIST.

That saith a spectacle for the ages, certainly, too deep for the thong-bound throng.

While he was doing our business elsewhere, I busied myself pouring the ale for our guests, and when he returned I also disappeared into the theater, sitting among the most scrunching shadows in the dimmest background. I too wanted invisibility, like the shadows within the deepest shadows.

I wanted to be simply an occurrence unobserved.

I was learning from my new hero, Grit, and I found that he resembled a man who builds bridges for a people whose religion is the denunciation of everything bridges might connect them to. And although I wondered why, I did not ask, because there was nobody to ask.

Undaunted by the tiny limits of reality the remembrance flicked through my consciousness that my favorite postcard had been an oddly still one, what I considered a distillation of zen balladry. It made me think of baskets nesting interminably.

    This card said,   FILIPENDULOUS,
                          FROM EARTH HANGS ONE TREE,
                          AND FROM
                          TREE ONE PERFECT PLUM.

It said enough.

    During the previous evening, before the movie's customers had arrived, Grit had shown me my new digs. It appeared to be obvious, even to so obtuse a fledgling as I was, that he was trying quite deliberately to bring me in without spooking me.

    He had shown me a couch in his apartment, in its own almost-alcove, that was become my personal bed, with a tiny closet which held shelves and a few bits of clothing which almost fit. They had been purchased in anticipation, I surmised. And I don't believe that anybody had ever anticipated me, in such a manner, before.

    And he had shown me the bathroom. And what a modern marvel is a bathroom! The toilet had its own water, and wasn't hooked up by a short length of cast-off rubber hose to the sink. And it had a bathtub, and it had a shower, and it had both cold and hot running water.

    Hallelujahs and hosannas, I was impressed! What luxury! God of my dreams had gleaned me! Unbegged questions had been answered gratis! Hot damn!

    Grit showed me where the towels were, and a small stack of my new clean underclothes, and how to use the faucets, and he told me to go do it. I walked in and he shut the door behind me, and I stripped and spent hours, at least, in the shower, loving it as the scalding rains cascaded over my face and down my chest and my legs. When I was done I toweled and dressed and opened the door and walked out a free man, so I thought, and found Grit waiting for me.

He said, "Let's look at you," and he spun me about and his eye darted in closely examining me, and he said, "Hmmrph. Okay, now let's try it using the soap and the shampoo."

He spun me back about and marched me back in, and carefully explained how to use the soap and the shampoo, which were strangers to me mostly. I had heard of soap being used to wash dishes, but that was the extent of my experience with it, almost. I had, I admit, used it to scrub the parts that showed, when I had cleaned myself a few times for company's sake, but that was it.

Shampoo was a word, only, I had seen used in advertisements.

But now I returned to the ablutions, and curried myself with a ton of suds, up and around. Then I dried and walked out to where Grit waited, a medallion of expressionless patience, and I stood before him naked as a tea-kettle shiny and new, and he was pleased.

"Excellent," he said, and I recalled his Moses-like commandment concerning cleanliness which had been only a matter of words when I had heard it, and I began now to understand it. I wondered if I too would develop hubris.

"Dress," he said, and he left.

And the night had begun, and the movie had begun and had ended, and I had slept on my couch, awakened only slightly as the few couch-dwelling stragglers had left from those other rooms and down the corridor of stairs whose doors led one way only.

And it was now a different bird had sung the day in.

Grit, when next I met him, told me that it was high time for us to begin our lessons. I had expected an advent of freedom, without any but pleasant responsibilities, so I was a bit crestfallen at this rather bleak news, and I suppose that something of my chagrin showed plainly on my face. As I mentioned earlier, I had never been an accomplished liar, though I do freely confess I did tend to envy such easy smiling fellows.

He said, "Today we begin as we will often begin," and he mentioned to me that there were in town certain very famous landmarks with which I ought to acquaint myself. On a table he laid a map of the city, and he pointed to ourselves, and he talked me through the city, carefully, deliberately, explicitly, explaining just how the map worked.

Then he pointed to a famous church, famous for its architecture, for its placement and its social history, and famous for a set of murals which adorned its courtyards. All of this he bade me discover, saying he wanted a complete description of everything I saw at the goal and of everything I saw on my way to the goal, and he wanted my reflections upon what I saw, my reflections upon my descriptions.

This of course represents Lord Chesterfield's directions to his son, in those famously cruel letters, and his intention was to bring his son's mind into existence outside of its boyish haze, and this was Grit's intention also.

My prospective journey was of some several miles, and after a breakfast which we shared, of tofu sandwiches with onions on whole rye bread, hot as hamburgers, with hot peppers and flax seeds and a tofu mayo, I set off. I had now a good shoe-leather beneath my feet, and I walked, stridingly, listening and watching, forcing myself into a relative interior stasis, becoming a spy, a conscientious divining rod.

Of course I could not understand that my such lessons were intended both to groom me to be a better companion for my future self, and to groom me for his pleasure in my companionship. And to be convenient for his use I must allow him his personal privacy, so he must send me on a long errands which would keep me effectually occupied.

"Benevolence without the discretion of selfishness would be intolerable," he might have said, idlingly. Often he appeared to understand things without needing to form words around them.

I did not require a benevolence lazing in altruism, and I went my little way as he directed. My chains did not chafe me, so I felt deliciously free. This was a new world, freshly plucked sizzlingly from the fires. Only in our youth can we feel such an exhilaration, and I was giddy.

When I returned to this little paradise I'd been expelled into, this builded cache inside my cornucopia, Grit asked me about my journey and its fruits. I told him about my trip to the famous church, and about my impressions of the murals he had asked especially about, and about my trip back to our home.

He asked, "What about the woman and the dog and the man, who were walking while obviously secure within a world of their own?" I pondered, for I had mentioned nothing of such a spectacle to him, and I pondered, and I remembered seeing just exactly such a sight. I could not for the life of me imagine how he had come to know of them, how he had seen with his eyes an image that had passed through my eyes, which I considered to be exclusively my personal territory.

My lower lip dangled like a pear from a neglected tree, and he asked, "What about the woman and the dog and the man?"   I said yes, that I had seen them, and were they special, and why were they remarkable, and what were they to him, and what to me?

He told me yes, and yes, and yes. He told me to ponder it, for they were vitally contemplable, and to ponder this matter until I understood it well, for he would ask me about it later.

And he said, "And what of that single building that stood with its backbone tall against the sun? Did you notice how the sun appeared to dwell beyond its windowpanes, bathing the world in psalms of light? That too was a holy cathedral, as holy as was the church you walked to see. Was one the better sight, the holier palace?"

He said, "I think not, perhaps."

I did not understand how he could know what I alone of us two had seen, and I watched him as if watching his face could help me to understand what I did not understand, but no information was available to me. I was embarrassed that he could so witness me, and yet I could feel the embarrassment dissipating slowly.

I was learning, and I knew that I was learning.

Grit asked me which of those visions I had seen impressed me the most, "Since it was not the woman and the dog and the man, and since it was not the spectral building homing the sun. And how might you convey to me what your favorite, your most daunting, your most answering vision, has meant to you?

"Can you draw it? Can you set in among a music? Could you sculpt it? Could you box it, or heave it?"

I did not know. My attempts at drawing had always been stickish and negligible, and I could produce no pleasantly musical noises either with my hand on paper or with my mouth in the wind. And I found myself to be inathletic, easily winded and readily distracted.

Grit examined the facial expression of my confounding, and the collapsed setting of my shoulders, and shrugged. He said, "Do you want some food," as he walked to the kitchen, and we shared bowls of chili with added yellow hungarian hot peppers, catfish, and shaved carrots. As he chatted, for he seldom talked business while he ate, he waved his bread in the air. He seldom talked bawdy at table, but he did always chat lightly, so that anyone might participate.

When we were through he and I washed the bowls, and pans, and he squared himself off toward me, saying, "Now comes a most important lesson," and he drew himself up to his full width. He was portly, like Hamlet.

He wasn't quite fat, but he was adequately material, and he could be an effective spectacle. I noticed that crowds always parted from his wending, dartingly like a smaller fish from a larger. He was pudgy, like Hamlet.

"Now is the time for you to clean the bathrooms. It is a good exercise for the well-being of your immortal soul. Clean the sinks and the toilets with an especial sedulous care, though this one time only, because you are new to it, you don't need to use your toothbrush to get the most difficultly distant spots. That will be later."

He must have his little joke, I learned later, though I did not know it then. And so he equipped me for this most humbling zen task, and so I cleaned those places and I cleaned them exceedingly well.

When I was through with such a labor for the soul I found him and he asked how I had done. "Did you do them well or ill?" he asked.

I had now begun to take his measure as a master, and I had found that he had in him no unkindness he was willing to distribute elsewhere than into his own psyche, so I replied, "They are excellently clean, sir. My toothbrush has too short a handle to reach those truly distant hidden recesses where the scum could linger, prosper, and proliferate, so I used your toothbrush instead." I said this with a face set entirely straight, knowing instinctively that a satire is aborted instantly if the smirk is displayed to the audience.

He looked at me with an evident curiosity, and he said, "And so, my youthful scoundrel, we have indeed discovered your appropriate milieu, the allotted hunting ground of your artistry. You are, of all misfortunate things, a satirist, a mimic of your betters. A detestable beast! O cruel misbegotten cynic! O wretch worming among the gutters of human depravity! O loathsome reptile..." He paused, and he laughed.

At first it was an intellectual chuckle, a selfconscious chortling, and then he began to laugh loudly and broadly, and his eyes sparkled. He was laughing at himself, and at my slightly bent characterization of his peculiar and ostensibly pretentious speech patterns, and then he began to cry great joyful tears and he bellylaughed into my face.

Then the well dried, almost abruptly, as he caught himself, and his garrulity caught up with him. He said, "You got me, little brother," and he laid his hand on my shoulders and we went in to eat, and we read, each in his own way.

Often Grit told me that boys would be boys, and must be boys, and knowing that I was theoretically absolved from working he realized that while he was working I would have time for other things which must be responsibly acknowledged.   If I were not assigned specifically to explore some distant church, or some distant mural, he would give me some similarly edifying assignment.

He told me that I must teach myself to think. He told me that I must teach myself to think and my fingers to speak. He told me that nobody knew his own thoughts until he had expressed them deliberately and elaborately, reasonably and imaginatively, intuitively and extrapolatively. Otherwise those thoughts remained in a smother.

He told me to learn to conduct my exercises amid people, because it was harder to think amid people than it was to think while alone, and that it was a more responsibly honorable endeavor, and a more accurate accomplishment.

Among his assignments, at very different times, was for me to walk to some distant bench beneath some distant tree, or where there were no trees, and to compose an essay on questions he specified.   What follows are a few of his peculiar assignments, his questions.

He asked me to discover, "What is the difference between thought and feeling?   And how does that difference apply for a woman, and for a man? Practicably speaking, what functional differences are caused by the very different physiological characteristics in the brains of women, and of men, and how might those differences determine behavior?"

He asked me to discuss on paper the various loci of organic creativity. How, he asked, do they differ between the feminine and the masculine? These centers include, he said, the ovaries and the testes, the female brain and its attendant nerves, the male brain and its attendant nerves, the female and the male heart, liver and the epidermis. What of the renal and of the splenetic? What do toes do when a poem occurs? How does a scent affect sculpting?

He asked me: At this moment of contemplation do you believe in God, or in god, or in GOD? Do you believe in Gods, or in gods? And what of this fantasy I posit: some enormous celestial Santa Claus draped in billowing whites, whose reindeer are angels, and whose reins subliminal commands? And what of Rudolph's red nose? Is the team's intended leader absent? Whose is the intended roof, and chimney, and tree? What is the function of the star upon the tree so conspicuously placed? What is the role of egoism in belief?

He said, "When I speak to you deliberately I withhold specific points of information because I understand that by withholding those specific points of information I provoke specific psychological configurations within the organism that is yourself. How do I do this, and why?"

He gave me a million books to read, each only when he believed because of his understanding of my abilities that I was prepared to receive the book approximately as it had been written, or as its purpose had best developed.

He asked me to contemplate the following preciously complicated poetical assertion: Draco was the potent hate of Athens exultingly made flesh, rendering visible the potent hate of sins, the potent hate of an intransigent egophagy. And while Grit asked, his ears laughed, shaking like trees in an earthquake.

He used words I could discover in no dictionary, words I could understand only by much exceedingly serious travail. It was a good hard fun, a bitter purgatory, and marvelously expansive.

It is easy for me to speculate that any average, any normal, any well-behaved person might tend to wonder that I did not submit myself to the scruples of any school. But what in this world would the schools have done with such a misaligned freak as I was?

The function of schools and of churches is to teach a massive obedience, to teach people to behave in ways that the society at large considers to be most lucrative. And I was genetically misaligned, so whether or not I sought the pains of individuation, they were mine to keep.

Grit was not wholly a scofflaw, and so it was that only sometimes, not quite often, when he'd send me on an edifying jaunt, he'd allow me to drive his battered pickup truck. I was not nearly able to drive legally, being approximately pubescent in age, so he cautioned me closely.

"Be always cautious when you drive, for with every revolution of wheels our family is imperilled, our destiny re-routed. Never listen to the radio, and never allow your mind to become a hum, but focus on your safety. A single error dooms us," he said.

Often I'd stop at a supermarket and gather our supplies. One dawny morning the skies lowered and drizzle shook itself over the town, and when I tried to park close to the market I found a brilliantly spanking new million-dollar sports car parked in the center of four parking-spaces, which forced me to park farther away in the drizzling dawn.

As I approached the market with an appearance of inadvertence I placed the sports car visually between myself and the market and my hand reached into my pocket and pulled forth a sharp steel can-opener, that

handy antique called a church-key. My steps held back
scarcely a bit, and yet when I had passed the car, deep
within its layers of paint and inscribed into its ribs of
steel was the single word, REPENT.

I had wanted to write, REPENT, ERE THE PRETTY
KNIGHT IS FALLEN, but deep graffiti ain't easy without a
powerful touch, and probably I'd have gotten caught by
the resident earthlings. That'd have been a bummer, I
thought in feeling.

Children can be devils because adults assume their
affectations to represent innocence, and by the time I
entered the store I was a palpable apparition of
innocence, smiling sweetly and humming a lullaby
almost. Every good salesman believes his own lies.

When my history is being perused it will of course be
noticed that Grit had a rather distinctive manner of
speaking, in that he was frequently more imaginative
than the situation appeared to require. I suspect that
his mind was only attempting to keep itself afloat, to
stave off boredom, to explore possible speculations.

Even his vehemence appeared to lack malicious
content, appeared to be only a vigorous exercise, like
taking the dog for a walk. In the earliest days of our
species when we walked our dogs our intent was to hunt
up a meal, and so it is today for commoner folks when
they unleash their vestigial imaginations.

We are the bastard spawn of gods and apes, I
reasoned.

Of course my friend Grit was no materialist predator,
much to his apparent disadvantage in our scheme of
things, and he was fond of goading temporally-enhanced
surface-dwelling materialist predators, while laughing.
He did not laugh only to provoke a laughing response,
and to avoid a beating, for, as he himself put it, "On our

battleground of human leather a man who wrestles timbers daily is likely to be an abler warrior than is a man who wrestles lies." Than a smiling liar is nothing smaller, I reasoned.

Once when he was feeling spunky, and perhaps a bit sadistic, like Cyrano, I heard him berating laughingly some temporally-enhanced surface-dwelling materialist predator. He laughed constantly, provoked by his own inventiveness, saying, "O you suppurating cold-sore on Satan's over-arching sphincter, what worms will choke upon your unclean carcass will be pariah'd by their more discreet peers! O you sewage-swilling shape-shifting subhuman excrement of robotic anguish! O nibbler of your bosses' unhallowed dingle-fruits! O leech! O plundering poltroon! O you running lesion of this dying universe! O impenitent sneaker-through of sublunary good! O you toadbanger, you pustulic seam-buster on all earthly stinkings! How fitter had your father been a sneaking onanist, you filthy sweat of bug-balls! You feast of vomit!"

He laughed all of the while he spoke, and yet he confessed to me later that he found it impossible not to be mightily offended by the folks who kill the world. He paused a moment, and he almost smirked, and he said, "Unless, of course, one happens to be recipient of an exceedingly generous largesse donated by one of those temporally-enhanced surface-dwelling materialist predators. Yes," he pondered, "I would enjoy an inabrogable sinecure," and his voice had trailed off to nothing, became invisible.

With women, in his displeasure, he was less gratifyingly self-indulgent, typically dismissing women drivers by calling them under his breath by that four-letter c word that women today extract such a perverse pleasure in despising.

Women of our eighteenth-century found a similar unhappy pleasure in being called audibly by the 5-letter b word, which he also used sometimes. Always he appeared to forget the instigations and the situations immediately, whereas I could brood upon them for days.

He was a good example not to follow, I thought at the time. As he once said self-mockingly, "I am not wholly worthless, since I can always serve as a bad example."

That evening for our supper we had tuna sandwiches on a whole cornmeal/wheat bread laced throughout with jalapenos, with tofu mayo and with mustard and with onions and clover sprouts. Grit had purchased approx 12 pounds of bananas for 10 cents per pound, and not all of them were wholly dark, so that was what we anticipated for breakfast and for lunch for the next day, etc.

I had been unused to such a peculiar fare when I had arrived, but was becoming accustomed to it. At Gimmy's and my mother's commonly I ate sandwiches of cheap mayonnaise on cheap white bread, with the mayonaise being considered the meat, I guess. And sometimes the mayonnaise was accompanied by a thick smear of lard.

But typically I had been offered whatever I might scrounge while cleaning the tables in the saloon and in the rooms above. In those rooms above the saloon the fare was sometimes a winner, consisting of dried half-burgers and dried french-fries.

And tomorrow night I knew we would have big steaming plates of freshly made whole wheat pappardelle with chunks of garlic and of banana, and with a delicious pesto sauce. And a bit of chicken.

Signals had been passed.

I have never been a heavy sleeper, and frequently I spin upon the bed throughout the night, my cat sedulously following my revolutions so as always to be realigned into my cradling arms and hands. And sometimes, I remember, I'd wake and realize I was alone in our apartment, realizing there was no breathing except mine and the cat's and no snoring.

I'd get out of bed, dutifully, and pad about and discover more consciously my aloneness, and I'd pad down the hall among the adjoining apartments. When Grit was to go a-visiting to his lady-friend, always he'd warn me because he knew I did not appreciate surprises, and on these other nighttimes I had not been warned to expect his absence.

A light streamed from the movie theatre, and by eager listening I could surmise what he was doing. And when, the following day, the task of cleaning up the area devolved upon me, that information I would glean also helped my surmises.

I could imagine Grit being unable to sleep, after I had retired, and he gave himself a glass of zinfandel, preferably a zinfandel fit to be shouted among the mountaintops by the old norse gods in boisterous revelry, Loki and his pals on a binge. Then, glass in one hand and bottle in his other hand, he'd go to the theatre.

On the big screen with himself the only audience would appear his favorite musical video recordings. And because he was lonely and male, typically these would be comprised of women singing. Indefatigably he had compiled sequentially chronological recordings that gave the illusion of being each a single concert. He had recordings of Emmylou Harris and of Tammy Wynette, and Alison Krauss, and of Helen Morgan. He had almost

4 hours of Billie Holiday, which is an ecstasy nonpareil. He had Patsy Cline, and Marianne Faithfull. He had Frank Sinatra, and Bob Wills, and Johnny Cash.

And he had Benny Leonard, and Charlie Chaplin.

My guess, based upon my personal observations, is that as the drink felled him he would become the swampborne monster that inhabits most men, Mr. Edward Hyde of Edinburgh, our individual prehistoric nemeses. And like good old Dr Johnson he preferred not to be witnessed as he devolved so thoroughly, with his only friend his cat.

Alcoholism is suicide, and periodic alcoholism, I reasoned, is a suicide on the installment plan. It is perhaps less abrupt than is a death by hanging, and is similarly masturbatory, self-indulgent, egotistic. It is childishly self-referential.

Fortunately, Grit had infrequent bouts.

The civilized bank of God.

Like a wagonload of cane dropping into some black-earth jungle down a long wet dangerous road, some portion of our lives was passed through. It was more than a hundred weeks, and it was fewer than a hundred months, and our selves changed as the earth changed.

We were poor, and yet the poverty because equably shared was seldom irksome. We were poor, and we dressed and were roofed poorly, and yet we were fairly comfortable.

Mostly we ate birds, because birds are cheap to eat unless people have almost no money at all. We ate steamed turkey necks with trenchers of brown rice. We ate platters of chicken gizzards which we had gleaned of their rich pouches of red-black meat (if we were feeling zennishly centered and wealthy. If we were feeling poorly we steamed them whole and ate them crunchingly, and tried not to be sullen and sulky,) with buckets of whole oats, or kamut, or barley.

And we ate buckets of beans, with oodles of sprouts, thick juicy mung sprouts, and thick juicy soy sprouts. We were not sufficiently poor to be miserable because of it.

As any patient daddy would do, when I was sick he'd nurse me with huge platters of brown rice noodled with freshly steamed onions, those big ones yellow on the outside and whose interiors appeared to be bursting with a green vitality. He'd say, "Let's see just how much your fine young belly can accommodate. Eat and yet eat, and pour down this gallon of good clear water," and he'd join me in my attack upon the rice and onions.

For butter we'd use a jigger of olive oil, and typically we'd include a fingerworth of salmon or of turkey. The oil that fell through would be rescued with pieces of whole grain rye bread, or a cornbread spiked with jalapenos.

And in a dutiful filial reciprocity I'd attend him when he was sick, and I remember once when he was sick he remarked, "I am unable to arrive. My brain is as dumbfounded as if it were merely a primordial spine and unable to debouch beyond the pineal. Forgive me if I appear to sulk, for I am as shy and as defensive as a terrapin."

Experience teaches us to understand strange languages, and I had mastered his language. "Enough brown rice can cure anything, almost, and yet it is the almost that frightens me," he said.

The deliria of exhausted dementia stagger toward a reasonableness, I thought, as if chaos would funnel itself into order. As I watched the spittle bubbling as he spoke, I was frightened in the distance, and with a napkin I wiped his lip, jaw, and chin. When I paused and smiled at him, trying to forestall any of his embarrassment, I was frightened.

Five of the seven days each week Grit would leave me and go to his necessary job, working as a laborer for a small lumberyard. Each evening like a father or like a brother he'd return, and it cost him a few minutes earnest meditation, a few minutes mediation with his personal gods, and then he would arrange his mind and become once again a human rather than merely another bitter cog. Being humane isn't easy for a sensitive, intelligent being, and requires an effort wholly real.

As always his bosses resented him frequently. They kept him employed only because he could become faceless occasionally, and because when they required an assistance of a special solid kind sometimes only he could offer it among their myrmidons. And they were all of them myrmidons to Mammon, and complained that when he was beside them they felt smalled, and such perpetually adolescent feeling made them bitter, and bitter.

And his lumberyard was sold, and when the previous owner left he absconded with a moiety of the retirement moneys though Grit had worked there for thirty years. Such depredations offered no recourse in this frenziedly cannibal society.

The building of our refuge, with its shops downstairs, and with its apartment and its theater in the upstairs, was duly sold, as the wagon rolled, and Grit and I found ourselves to be free men. Only the homeless and the dead are free, and we were free.

Certainly it is that a being who could with a blow create our whole teeming universe, could in a little while bring the rains upon a barren field and flood the plain with flowers, each of its kind. And how exceedingly presumptuous would be that flower who pretended to understand the universal design and to comprehend the mind behind it.

And so I do not suspect that I ever did know my

father, and I never did suspect that Gimmy was he. Gimmy told me once, "Your father's days were rung with stars, and his nights bloomed in ecstasy, the deadly ecstasy of the damned. He never saw a sober day, and he never saw a sober night." I do not believe I ever did see Gimmy sober.

When Grit told me it was time to go, I knew instinctively it was time for us to go. He did not need to specify our unity, since I had accepted him as my father and my brother: he was my home.

When the almighty fates conspire to run you out of town is a good time already to own a pickup truck, however seedy and leaky round the edges, and however frail in its guts. Grit extricated from the basement of our apartment building a weathered, battered old camper shell, and we filled it with whatever he could not bear to abandon. That means our cat, a few books, a few videos just in case, a few records ditto, some sleeping and some clothing gear. He never ate canned food except for fish, so we took his tuna and sardines.

We took some bottles of wine, of peanut butter, of salsa.

Grit was the world's most private man, and while we were packing the telephone rang. He stopped, and like a huntingdog in the field he stood at point, watching the telephone as it continued to ring. Had he been an eye in the sky he might have reminded himself of those famous photographs of folks during World War 2 listening to Franklin Delano Roosevelt's fireside chats and watching their radios.

After the designated number of rings, which was 6, he heard his answering machine recording the voice of one of our neighbors who shared these lofty apartments in our building. He kept our phone in a closet, as if it were like a toilet used during scenes which some overly-fastidious people considered to be obscenely embarrassing, and instantly he stepped into the closet and he closed the door securely behind him, so my tender ears could not hear his discussion.

But I had heard him and her numerous times before, and had been with her and with both of them in her apartment. She was a few years older than he, and because she was lonely she was friendly. I had encountered her in our communal hallway on a few occasions when first I had arrived, and we had chatted comfortably, and she had invited me to visit her. When I had visited, she had served tea and she pushed our chatter in his direction, if she and I were alone.

I had long since learned that the precocity of prodigies frightens folks, and that in an unnecessary attempt to defend their egos common folks translate their fear into anger and sadism, so when I spoke with her I was careful not to be viewed. I would speak noncommittally those innocent meaninglessnesses which I supposed she wanted to hear.

And I spoke what she wanted, which was of him.

I found it immensely entertaining to discover that she was fond of referring to people she disliked, who were legion, as being poor white trailor trash. One suspects that in an earlier country she would have aimed at the gypsies, referring to folks on the go.

On early mornings she would brew a pot of chinese gunpowder, bitter green tea so strong I'd choke as I sipped it, and afterward I'd feel as if my brains were stirred with a stick. Sometimes the tea interfered with my ability to process my perceptions, sometimes resulting in confusion, in fear or in anger.

On her deck she had a hot-tub and for deckposts she

had thirteen carven statues, fishy-looking sculptures representing the apostles and Mary in the fetal state. In her mind, I thought, she must certainly accuse GOD of having consciousness, and of having an exceedingly personal interest in herself. Her deity was a manifestation of the verb "to have", as mine was of the verb "to be", sometimes. For some people it is "to do".

She had cats Judas and Jesus, who were cautious allies with our cat, god. She had four parrots, Eenie, Meenie, Minie, and Moe, who were as interesting as any people I had encountered, almost, honorable little creatures a bit too tightly wound, who'd frolic among the kitties imperviously, teasing them and cavorting like monkeys. Occasionally the parrots and the kitticats would crawl together under the bedcovers, wheelingly.

She had bigger rooms than we had, a palatial warren, and she liked the oddest decorations. She preferred newspapers to paintings and to photographs of the typical kind, and one room was decorated as a shrine to Fred Astaire, with framed newspaper pages of his exploits adorning the walls. Another room was a shrine to Abraham Lincoln, also with framed pages. In her bathroom beside the throne was a scrapbook she had collected of curious newspaper articles, my favorite being about a grizzly bear in a Seattle zoo who in his loneliness had adopted a kitten.

In her diningroom was a framed newspaper page which included a fictional story written by Grit under an hispanic pseudonym. She commented that the San Francisco Chronicle, which published the story, would never have published it had they known the writer was a honkie male. I did not dispute her sophistication.

Arguing with women betrays weakness, I thought.

She at least had never called me Working Boy.

On her deck she had an open terrarium, and a nine-inch box turtle she called Clit Tortoise. Only once had I picked it up, and had been rewarded with an instant spurt of urine that nailed me from tit to toenail. She had laughed at my discomfiture, of course. She was good at laughing, and because no malice lurked in her laughter her laughter made me laugh.

Periodically in her alcoholism she would expose herself to the nightwinds, while boozing upon her deck or with her windows wide, and pneumonia would fill her lungs with fluids and her mind with hallucinations. Soon someone would summon the police and the police would summon an ambulance, and she would be carted away for a month or for a few months.

And after her return a year would pass or two years would pass, and the unhappy event would recur, item by item. The hallucination was an event as fixed as the earth that falls around the sun: always she was being attacked by hordes of small dark men.

In our privacy I had asked Grit why he visited her occasionally, and he said, "Sometimes the blood is up and I must go. She transcephalates my blood and the horn is sounded through the forest, and I must seek a brief captivity beneath a tree. I am become a unicorn awhile."

Obviously he chose not to communicate more precisely. He often sought refuge in metaphor. But I was on the crest of puberty, and understood ably enough.

And in those times he would leave our apartment, communicate with her as she and he required, and he would return.

Sometimes when we three were together she would attempt an argument, because she must, and he would exclaim, almost playfully, as if gently beseeching, "O please do stop being a woman. Come to me, and let's espouse each other as a pleasantness. Don't espouse causes polemically in this brief space we share. We are friends, and being friends we do not require the aggravation."

She would look sharply at him, and without any appreciable movement some emotional corollary to her sinews would shrug, and she'd smile as if with a special secret she shared only with her feminine ancestral blood, some distant relative to what we might call pity. Perhaps she communicated with some ancestral fire-breathing hag whose coven controlled some ancient millenium.

And then the cloud cleared, amiably enough.

And on this occasion as we were packing, he had stepped into the closet upon realizing it was she on the phone. And now the door opened, and he held the phone in hand, and I heard him say distinctly, "O please do stop acting like a woman. You know how it confuses me," and he chuckled. And laughed.

He did not chuckle to me or for himself, but as a communication to her, acknowledging that something was understood amenably, was forgiven. His propulsive requirements satisfied, he put down the phone and he closed the door.

We continued packing. His facial expression had already forgotten the conversation, and his mind was following his face, as he directed it to do. He glanced back once as if to glance through the door, through the phone and the intervening lines, and into her rooms. He did not glance twice.

I was watching, so I know.

Lambs by a pen released.

Grit loved pockets, and always he wore a teeshirt that had a pocket or 2, and his shirts all had 2 breast pockets and perhaps other pockets elsewhere. He turned to me and he said, "What book do you take?"

I replied, "We've packed a hundred books."

He said, "I meant, What book do you take on your person?"

"What," I said.

"Always," he said, "you should carry some tiny volume, one that is your friend, that is inexhaustible. I carry TONY AND CLEO. My father during his warring tucked Edward Fitzgerald's translation of Omar, somewhere in his pack, everywhere. Once upon a time I carried TITUS ANDRONICUS, but it was too brisk, and years earlier I carried HAMLET until I found the wall gave back no reflections.

"Every man needs a friend, especially if it cannot be he."

And we continued to pack, a labor of an hour drawn out to a few slow hours. Clearly we did not wish to go, though we did choose to go. I did suspect he was hoping for intervention, some god-on-a-trolley to save the show with a windfall of manna precisely placed.

But miracles happen only to the dead.

As we drove away I pondered silently upon this my latest fateful year. Puberty had struck, and my voice was nearly as deep as was Grit's voice that strode between bass and baritone. But physically I was much smaller than he.

He was about 6 feet tall and 225 pounds, and though his shoulders were not wide they were massively thick, as was his gigantic chest. He told me once that a fellow laborer at the lumberyard had accused him of possessing no neck, and once I had watched as a man larger than he had mocked Grit's wholesale penury and with one hand Grit had raised him by his belt buckle and with his other hand had lightly tickled his facial features, repeatedly, causing such frustration and humiliation the other man had begun to cry. Grit had then let him softly down, patted him on the head, and about the ears, and had stepped away.

And now we were off. I did not ask, but I did suspect that we had but small moneys, and Grit had told me that our neighbor had given him several large bills as a token of farewell. She had chosen her parents well, and financially was comfy.

In the car we listened to no radio, since the car was almost antiquey and the radio had broken years ago, and Grit hated ill-tuned radios anyway. We brought an accurate portable radio, and a few cassettes. But silence was our norm.

My status was by now an equivocal one, and I suppose I considered myself to be professionally a slipper-through-the-cracks. Grit supported me by his daily labors, and yet I figured it behooved me to contribute my small somethings to our material endeavor. I did not go to school, except to his very specific and arduous unofficial school which consisted of much waiting and watching and studying, and of much reading and of questioning, and of much contemplation and of much discussion with my principal mentor, and so I had a bit of time on my hands occasionally when he was at his work.

And, clearly contrary to what we as a society have been programmed to believe, many many children, rural and urban, do not acknowledge the official system by an attendance at some life-blistering school where, inevitably, folks are instructed in the arts of being equably insincere rather than in the cosmic duty of attempting to understand truth and to abide by that understanding despite societal restraints.

And so I too spent much time by working, much as I had always done at least since the advent of consciousness, and some of my workings would not have been deemed to be criminal by the authorities. And I spent much good time cleverly slipping through the cracks, being unobtrusive.

So when Grit suggested that we would continue to rely upon our hard labors, I was undisgruntled, for I had been there before, a time or three. When we stopped our beat-up old toyota for meals we engaged freely in the restaurant chatter just in case something chanced to turn up, in the Pickwickian sense, because a man cannot live without money.

Work is an important meaninglessness, except when it is good hard fun and a cruel joy. To appreciate work is a wisdom, and wisdom is a bitter virtue, I thought.

Grit and I shared the tedium of the roadway, as we shared most things which greeted our lives, and though I had no driver's license I did my full share of the driving. To beguile the tedium we spoke poetry at each other, with him using one contemporary and favorite poet, and with me then responding with a dead and favorite poet, or vice versa.

We remembered reading that a favorite cocktail party trick of the famous actor, Richard Burton, was to recite any of Shakespeare's sonnets upon request, and to recite it backward. We remembered reading that that old scribbler of the american democracy, James Madison, was reputedly able to translate into Latin with one hand, and to translate into Greek with his other hand, what was being spoken in English at the moment.

Definitely we could do neither of those feats, but I did have down pat the crashing cadence of THE SECOND COMING, and sometimes I would assail Grit with that gem, or with Vachel Lindsay's THE CONGO, whose musical intensity I could never quite divest myself of, also.

He asked that I hail him with something I had written myself, and being a bit of an egotistical shill, a ham certainly, I responded with what duly follows. I have never discovered quite where it came from, or quite what it meant, though I did understand that it meant.

"In the beginning was the tail collective, and in the early lives of our created species we had long ropy tails. These resembled, because of the resemblance of species, the tails of monkeys but ours were much better and much more useful. Ours were not merely vestigial things, runted abstractions of something much greater than themselves, but had in them almost an infinity of individual and of collectively organized nerves and muscles stranding into wholeness of purpose. These tails were remarkably longer than we were tall, sinuous.

"Sometimes in an eruption of chance we might be found sitting like blackbirds on a wire fence, our tails being so perfectly wrapped round each other in almost an endless line, or making toward a circle of many or a circle of two. And endless fibrillations, but in a perfect unanimity of purpose, passed valuable informations back and forth along that convenient tentacle, resulting in a complete knowledge among all recipients.

"Then we were a unit truly.

"But something happened to change this ideal of humane existence, and caused us to be severed. Perhaps it was that one among us yearned for some special recognition, and was accorded it to the detriment of all of us, and our collection was broken, as the tails removed. Perhaps somebody among us spoke the poisonous word?

"I dunno."

Grit had an exceedingly disconcerting habit, in that commonly he laughed in much the same manner as he cried, which is to say, silently. Our psychological health demands that laughter and tears be similarly social contrivances, apparently, and it is bothersome when somebody laughs or cries and declines to share the exuberance with anybody else. That niggardliness is egotistic, selfish, and causes the audience to feel cheated. It embitters the audience, whether reasonably or unreasonably.

And so it was now. I had spoken my piece, and now felt almost as self-containedly farflung as Rimbaud must have felt when he spoke his psychedelic intricacies to Verlaine, his pal with dishonest eyes.

We continued to drive for a minute or so, an excruciating minute for me, and I dared not look full at Grit, so I ignored him and gazed at the scenery, and I felt rather than heard, though hearing is feeling, the beginning of a chuckle. He was chuckling without a sound. It was almost unnerving.

He said, "And is that not a rather precipitate descent from the sublime to the ridiculous. You soar almost upward with spirits on the go, and then to reassert your earthliness you squat upon a rotten leaf and plop to land, a banal immersion.

"Whatever will I do with you? You are a grouchier bug than I, even, and your discreetly caustic irreverence is more acid than mine, even. And yet behind an expression of childlike mildness you hide your wit and your meanness," he speculated.

Surely he was too hard by half. Surely I had merely been beguiling the time, the tedium, but what is guile? Surely he was too hard, and I had always been misunderstood. Is guile a mere beguiling?

Once again I had recourse to retreat into subterfuge, to dissimulate incomprehension, to feign ignorance, and I said, "It is perhaps unkind, and it is certainly ungenerous, to mock my humbly offered TALES I HAVE BEEN HANGED BY. It had been offered in good sound spirit, and you gutter it and me together in a bitterness that smacks of a smallness I do not understand."

I had learned well from my master.

He replied, ostensibly apropos of nothing, "You have learned well from a master. Mano a mano, you are a shifty beast."

Neither of us was fooled even a bit, and yet the discussion terminated, as such discussions often must terminate when they begin to become too unpleasantly accurate and the sight of the tether is lost.

We scooted across the endless plain, after we had left the water and wavered across the mountains which are hills. The plain was flat as a pan, and stable.

Because the mind is finite a plane continues until it encounters the solution that is itself again, and it is rolled into a planet, a sphere with an imperfect surface. An infinite mentation, whether a mind or otherwise, would accept without demur the final inutility of solutions, and the plane could roll forever flat.

And so it was that we traveled on a plain, and we never quite lost ourselves, and eventually we found ourselves in a town upon a plain. One sign duly proclaimed a restaurant, and so we stepped in for a bite of chow. One might suppose that the restaurant had a name, but we did not find that name, and we did not find the name of the town, nor of the plain. It was the same with us.

So this, I thought though not quite in words, was where we get the expression, a greasy spoon restaurant. It was a big block of a building, and once we had landed inside of it we could see the okie decorations everywhere, consisting of hunting trophies, antlered trophies with glazed eyes and slightly lolling tongues, colored lightbulbs near the ceiling as if in preparation for a perpetual christmas, a glassed and boxed collection of whipsockets.

The maitre d' was a big old country boy, fat as a turkey's tail, sporting a freshly bleached undershirt boasting a pack of Camel's rolled up in the sinister sleeve above a tattoo of somebody's Pope smoking a cigar above the caption FATHER KNOWS BEST. His skull was wrapped with fat and was as big as a bison's.

As we sauntered in he was pleasantly informing a patron that "though you're the fuzz on my peaches you wouldn't know beans from rice if the bags were opened." He laughed constantly as if it were an emotional leakage, a physiological slippage.

Whether in response to the movement of the door or in response to ourselves personally, he turned his attention toward us, tracking us with his eyes as we moved toward and as we intercepted a table and we sat. As if we were his recently discovered brothers he said, "Hi fellas," and he lowered his voice a thousandth of a notch to confide stagily, "This fine day our specialty is a chicken-fried steak. The meat's so tender I don't see how the cow could move, moove, mooove, moooove," and his fat jaw jutted forth and swung in a low flat arc like the cowcatcher on an old western choo-choo train going round a bend. His impressive amplitude of chins followed his jaw as it began the movement and they continued to pendulate slowingly after it had stopped.

His tiny piggy eyes leapt sparklingly and they shuttered round the room to invite everybody to partake of his jollity. Clearly it was one of his standard lines and everybody laughed amiably, knowing his tunes.

Quietly but clearly Grit suggested that perhaps the cow had been able to afford a chauffeur. The little piggy eyes stopped laughing, but the lungs laughed through the drooly mouth.

Cunning is jealous, I thought.

We sipped the coffee, neither Jamaican or Celebesian. Occasionally, as the big old boy shouted orders to the kitchen, a giantess would stuff her self through the communicating aperture and survey the room amiably. Her hairs ranged from reds through yellows, blues through greens, with a generous display of pink scalp.

When she guffawed her assembled toothsomeness was a rainbow of yellows and salmons and blacks-and-blues, except for numerous deletions where paled the phantom chompers. Our steaks were passed from her massive paw to his massive paw, and we surfeited on ripe misnomered tender slabs garnished with succulent fresh avocadoes and parsley whisks, shavings of carrot. The fries were from fresh whole potatoes with skins attached, thick as a giant's fingers, tender as a child's feelings.

Around us as we sat and as we ate the hubbub sounded and resounded buffetingly. The gathering noise was claustrophobic and we could not help but to hear the mindless din, the mindless humming of an incessant chatter. The jolly maitre d' was casting his jokes wildly, seemingly, like the smoke from a padre's censer. The noise was cutting us off from the crowd and we existed in our special cosmos, contemplating ourselves, as if the noisy atmosphere resembled the thick dark air during a snow or during a heavy rain that had been chasing the earth for days and had finally got it into a corner and was closing in.

Our personalities almost never clashed between themselves, but rather stirred within a common assumption. He asked, "Sometimes you must wonder how I got myself into this grand petty personal mess that is mine. My life has always been an oppressive jungle and I the only thing that crawled or wove among the branches and the droppings of the wet, and once I only wanted its absence.

"I loved a woman as only a desperate man can love a woman, and I have reason to believe it was reciprocal, for reasons I cannot say," and he continued in his softest of softest voices, yet hard and unrelenting as any unconscionable truth expressed by disembittered gods.

She had been wanted also by another man who had been better born, who had paid him money for renunciation, and Grit who had been desperate had accepted these moneys not unwillingly, these tinkling moneys like this the music of the keys. I did not pretend I did not understand.

"What became of her I know," he said. "Love is more precious than glass."

He did not say diamonds.

Sheep masquerading as lambs.

We rode on, seemingly endlessly while it was occurring, never galloping. I said to Grit, "May I tell you about a dream I had," and he said, "Certainly, and in course I will tell you with an equal seldomness of some dreams I have had, as they appear."

"I was living in a house which was a home, with my father and with my mother and with a dog, a happy golden retriever, and I was happy. My father was nice and my mother was nice, and the niceness rolled through us as if were an atmosphere that could not end. A succession of meaningless vital things happened, and we were careful with each other.

"Without specific delineations my mother and my father imploded, or just disappeared, moved through appearance to disappearance like a mist on a mirror. I was called through the doorway, and I moved through the doorway, and I noticed that the door was now broken in a place just beside the doorknob.

"I knew that our dog remained inside the house, and I was determining not to abandon the dog who had become old and angular. The decision was a conscious decision, although I continued to be in the process of leaving through the doorway. Somewhere the human angels of my consciousness were singing the carol, O TANNENBAUM, amid a small orchestra.

"I had abandoned the dog who had loved me, as I had loved him.

"I had no memory of any cruelties perpetrated by my mother or by my father, and I remembered only healthy smilings and intimate kindnesses, and yet they had abandoned me." I silenced.

"They had no rememberable faces."

Grit said, "It is too easy to blame ourselves for the injuries others have done us, and it does not help. Orphans must become adults or their bewilderment is meaningless in our long scheme. I suspect our pal Marcus Aurelius might help us at this juncture, better than I, and at our leisure it might be useful to consult such a happy pragmatist. What an improvement to be happy without being foolish!

"Tonight at our campfire we will summon his book-bound genie across the fitful leagues. Genius talks, and it is well," and he looked and smiled at me. I was grateful he had no condescension, and had already begun to realize that friendship cannot survive condescension.

Friendship is an escape from ego, I thought.

His voice arrived as if it had walked a long journey across the mountains, or up from some distant valley buried by mighty oceans, "Now you feel in safety you believe your mother and your father, who is the more elusive character in your pictures, were for you predators and you were prey, and yet it is as similarly true that you were the parasite and they served in the capacity as a host. Unequal and stressy symbioses cannot be pleasant but they may be vital, as when we place upon a stage the hyena and the lion and we realize that deprived of that necessary structuring some greater predator might have appeared compared to whom those two formidable beasts are but as puppets, as toys for the dawdlings by babies.

"We will think on this matter, and it will come to us more clearly," he said, and we were silent.

Victors and victims, I mused.

Miles we drove and miles farther we drove seemingly endlessly, sipping our waters and sipping the tea which brewed endlessly in a great jug held in the cargo bin back of the truck. We chatted sometimes concerning the map which our designated passenger kept by his lap, chatting almost aimlessly about places mentioned we had never been.

A small public lake approached us, preparing us of its arrival by a series of roadsigns each displaying a lesser mileage than had its predecessor, and it was decided to camp for the night, to let the dark spell pass. The lake had a brief available beachfront and we made a fire. We cooked grub, and we washed in the public restrooms. The stars too had arrived.

The big bad old night was hunkering down around us, crowding us.

We scrounged perhaps illegally that evening and we constructed a small campfire and we steamed artichokes. Grit told me that artichokes were a soulfood for him, bringing him peace, and I was bound to appreciate anything he appreciated. It was easy for me to be grateful that he had accepted such a burden as I, and I was grateful.

Our perceptions are reflected in our behavior, I pondered.

After the artichokes and the whole rye bread, and the artichoke tea, we sat complacently, mingling in our equable thoughts. He mentioned that we as a species and as tribes had always believed in things we were too small to comprehend, and that we tended to create gods and aliens in our ostensible images easily.

Perhaps the artichokes had been undercooked, or perhaps a miasma moved through the slightly scudding breeze, but something caused our tentative minds to move. Perhaps it was simply a tendency of our living humanity, that tendency that caused our ancestors to cross mountains in response to tenuous rumors, that tendency to covet a new ring of neighbors elsewhere, our human restlessness.

Sitting we chatted, in our natural intimacy neither of us embarrassed or feeling any need to hide, any need to peek or not to peek. We were as brothers ought to be, and in neither of us would consciousness be still. Movement announces vitality, I suppose. "Form must move or be dead, and the urge that necessitates form must behave similarly," I thought, in the ready decisiveness of youth.

It was a spatial thing, I suggested, looking.

Our minds became restive as we sat after supper, after desultory chatting, and the sounds of wild night hemmed us in. I commented that the night was closing in on us, and he commented, capriciously perhaps, that all of our material world consisted only of curtains which surrounded us, and that the materialist-slipping extraterrestrials were cascading toward us from points unknown to us, their conveniently assumed bodies or ships bulging the material fabric from the distant ground.

Though he may have been wryly facetious I

shuddered inwardly at the conceit, thinking it odd that humans could find ourselves so desirable or so interesting, that we as humans could so fascinate ourselves. He applauded when I suggested that those tremors in the fabric to which he alluded more closely resembled the slight bulgings caused by a woman's fingertips clutching the curtains while she watches through the curtains a man departing on the distant side, as he glances back toward her and then disappointedly climbs into his car perhaps. Curtains are closed, very.

Perhaps with her other hand she raises her fingertips tentatively, gently with a small sad fear, and she waves her fingertips individually almost, as if they communicate imprecisely among themselves, I suggested. He inquired, "What of her lips and eyelashes?"

I smiled uneasily.

Our cat, god, stirred under my fingers, looked up at my face and barked softly, smiling felinely. I asked Grit if he believed in the presence of extraterrestrials, and in extraterrestrials themselves.

He replied, "Sometimes I do. Otherwise it is difficult to explain the Andes, and potatoes, corn, amaranth, quinoa. Dragons and the yeti are easily explained, but not potatoes. My mind vacillates."

"It is well to speak carefully sometimes, I suppose," I asked him, after a longish pause, "and I ask you to tell me what you picture when you imagine one of our extraterrestrial visitors."

Slowly like a slowly unwinding snake he spoke, "It won't help our process to explain that our concepts of singularity and of multiplicity may be wrong, or may be inappropriate.

"Let me say that, accepting your assumption of

singularity, I picture a face like the face of a crab, and my eyes unfocus to a haze where I suspect the occurrence of tentacles or of leg-things.

"We believe in the inevitable realities of air, earth, fire, and water, and their realities appear unbroachable to us. I do not believe that every being would find our matter unbroachable, despite our religious shouts. And I suspect our human mind is easily blasted."

The night settled as our contemplations gentled.

I said, "What do you picture when you contemplate gods, regardless of the size of your gees, or not regardless?"

He said, "I place no bodies around my visions, big g or little g, or any of the gees in between and on either side. Bedtime nighs, my peripatetic existentialist..."

And the images we promulgate are always physical images, since we are unable to imagine the constructions of psyche which we embody also. I said, "Do you suggest that we have actually created in our own image those representations of aliens and of gods which have so fired our popular and mythological storyings?"

"And that they have no realer existence than ourselves?" he continued.

"Created yes they must have been created as certainly as we had been created beings, but what on this earth compels us to believe or to suspect that they had been created in our discernible image?

"Even if the event produced or revealed only the proper number of arms and legs and heads, how could we have anticipated the occurrence reasonably, or responsibly? Every such effort, surely, is merely our superstition? I ask.

"Every such anticipation reflects the boldness of our smallness? I only ask. Who is qualified to say? What occurs when the brain contemplates itself?"

Surrounding us the night awoke again and the sounds shuffled. Through the interpreting haze of evening and of campglow I could see the waters we camped beside, the sheeted laking of the water. Fish punched the surface lipping mosquitoes, and retreating.

"I confess this is a bit heavy for my wee human noggin," I murmured, as I teased the dwindling embers with a stick, watching the coruscating tip. "I haven't your ease, your facility," I said, and I think that last word stung him.

He replied after a patient pause.

"Heavy matters because they are profound wash downward to greater harder depths than do their lighter, easier cousins, and like the primeval inhabitants of the waters' abysses they straggle interminably while things lighter and flightier are swept away in the fitful course of agings.

"It improves us when we try to understand," and he stilled.

Life's continuum evolved, as the world rolled below us on its seemingly endless march, and it was glad for me to watch as those individual lines of failure were slowly erased from my friend's face, and from his movement. Alcohol, and alcoholism, and even a controlled or a repressed alcoholism, disrupts the blood and flays the face from the skull until the face hangs like an ill-used drapery, grotesquely.

Alcoholism imagines monsters when there is but one, and it is ourself. Alcoholism creates monstrosities of behavior and of perception, and our brief hiatus had begun an amelioration. My friend's face was reattaching to his skull, and assuming his wonted expressions. He was calming.

He slept often. Some evenings we'd bed down at 8, and it was 8 again ere he'd stir. Come mornings by that time I had cleaned our site, and had cleaned myself, and had secured a breakfast and a read.

I enjoyed wandering the little stations we visited, just to listen and to watch. I enjoyed browsing the local paper, which I picked from benches and from cans and from idle tables. Humans are so painstakingly meaningless, so mean and so unexpectedly generous, gallant and treacherous, honorable and selfish! What damned difficult fun!

It ain't easy not being dead.

If the world were perfectly round we'd all be strolling downhill, I thought, blaming the irregularities for all the climbing and the falling, and the landing.

In the morning the new world shone almost cloudfree and the bashful sun lent a pleasant cheer. I prepared our simple breakfast, including a local paper only a few days old, and a clutch of napkins we had acquired. From the truck I disentangled a tattered boyish fishingpole and with a skewered grub I toyed at the lakeside.

Our companion, god, added his ineffable insights and comments, hoping for leviathan. He said, "Let us always eschew the nontraditional. It is now an excellent opportunity for your fingertips to tickle my tummy," so I complied dutifully. Cats tend to be imperious, fortunately.

As I was battling in a trout almost as long as my long finger, and landing the beast accompanied by god's rather too ironic applause, Grit sauntered over and watched, concealing his admiration ably. He looked as glamorous as an overflowing clothes-hamper in a dirty closet might look on a hungover morning to the residents of an unkempt old-folks' home while the ill-paid caregivers shuffle them toward the toilets. His hair was sticking at all angles and he had eye-boogers and his clothes were unbuttoned, unzipped, and stained with sweat and earth's grime.

Even the fish belched in embarrassment.

He sat and we drank coffee, he hugely.

Whining, snuffling, and whimpering sounded, and god ran off. Of course being a cat god could not run to the truck, which would have been a course too reasonable. Reasonable behavior would insult the gods of the world, so they act creatively: each is individuated and original, without pretense, much as creatures become gravely ill without pretense.

A one-eyed, buck-toothed dog weaseled up to us, as morningly ugly as Grit himself, and Grit immediately named him Jingo. Now we were, I suspected, 4 mutts on a pilgrimage.

Magnanimously, and because it was too small to be of use, I released the little trout, and Grit and I had our breakfast, which consisted of leftover artichokes and a wee bit of yellowtail tuna he had finagled. As was typical, his tooth-scraped leaves he deposited on his plate in one perfectly aligned sequentially-constructed arc. Once he informed me, upon my inquiry, that his arc was the beginning of a spiral, not the beginning of a circle.

Jingo was delighted to receive some chicken skin, fat, and meats. Apparently he had been attemptedly eaten by somebody, because he had tooth marks and claw marks along his visible spine, and occasionally he trembled unwittingly. He smiled at us unreservedly, assuming, apparently, we would be his home. But could Jingo and god be friends?

Our feeding complete for the nonce, we strolled a bit

away from our campsite and we swam, luxuriously, dunking ourselves and dunking one another. We dried, then, Jingo rattling his wet sparks on everything, and I resumed my angling.

Grit climbed into Immanuel Velikosky's WORLDS IN COLLISION, a natural choice for a man who had joked that his hometown had been Charles' Fort and he had graduated from Endorphin High. Occasionally he would snort as he discovered a logical fallacy or a failure of adequate considerations.

The gunny-sack I had tied into the water was appropriately filling with small and acceptable trout, and toward the noon I asked if he wanted to head on out anytime soon. He understood that I was suggesting we proceed, and he replied, "If you continue to fish so successfully, we'll be able to feed all of the 4 of us. Our neighbors are few and they distant beyond the reach of shrieks. Those polyphemic robots who feed the damned, those catatonia-inducing lights of the blue brainkillers, those black holes of the mind, those... televisions are invisible to us, and radios are invisible to our ears. Why go? Why go?

"When we can be content without going we defeat our brutishness, and going is always a fugitive thing. Let's only circle our wagons for awhile, till necessity compels, and then we'll go," he decided.

Jingo was pleased. I was happy, although god had absquatulated, apparently, and Grit was delved and opened once again in his survey of Velikovsky's miltonic cosmic battlings. He sounded like a sleeping kitten as he wrestled, not with the book, but with the writer.

We stayed at the campsite for some while, many days. Our sweet kitticat god had disappeared, doubtless because of the appearance of the dog, Jingo. That was depressing, and distressing, especially for god, I supposed. I told Grit, who was casually in mourning for our god, "Our world revolves from gods to dogs, and perhaps back again, over and over, and it is a necessary calamity."

Grit glanced at me wryly, disapproving of my mood because my moods were too easily a mirror of his moods. He had said my moods were his moods, as seen "through a glass, dungly." He had not smiled, even falsely.

He was never rife with compliments.

"Whom had we been entertaining unaware? Might it have been an ...?"

One day past noon we heard a stertorous clacking, and a billowing old flatbed truck appeared and chaboogled over beside our truck, and coughed until it stilled. Immediately upon hearing its consumptive noisings, Jingo had run and hidden in some bushes.

An old battered red-necked man, looking farmerish, climbed out and asked if we had seen his dog, and he described Jingo rather exactly, neglecting to mention only the dog's incessant smilings. Being an orderly fellow my answer was to turn a deadpan face to Grit, who denied having seen any dog but inquired if the farmer had seen our cat, whose name was Hooligan.

The farmer temporized and gazed about, pretending not to notice various doggy contributions to the landscape which lay freshly scattered in the vicinity. I thought that him being a farmer and therefore a hunter it was likely he could identify his dog by his dog's poop, and I said nada. His eyes asked me if Grit lied, and mine replied that I was too obtuse to see the query.

He plopped down before my feet, from the back of his truck, which he called his bobtail, a great gunnysack of green fallen walnuts, and told me to toss it in the exposed cargo-bin of our pickup for awhile till they cured and could be shucked. He gave us a few heads of cabbage and some potatoes, said he'd be back and to hold his dog if it showed.

Clearly he considered Grit to be a liar, and he considered me to be a liar's confederate, or maybe only a fibber since I had actually denied nothing verbally. And he rode off into the sunset.

As soon as the billows were no longer visible, and his truck could be considered as being scarcely more than a fading metallic shout, Jingo popped back among us and began barking his contempt for his erstwhile master, tormentor, and chef.

My imagination conjured the prospect of a single bang, and a dog dead, but fortunately I was only borrowing troubles once again. The bobtail faded into silence, and we 3 remained.

"Perhaps those vegies were his," I thought curiously. Every morning while Grit slept I prowled the neighborhood of the lake, looking for advantage and finding some. Yes, there were plowed fields.

"Perhaps," I thought, "his wilful contribution is not intended only as a bribe but as an appeasement. Our perceptual mechanism is defensive and he was watchful as a hungry snake.

"He wants Jingo, thinks we have him. He wants his farm, thinks we are stealing it in nibbles. Next comes the gun. Oops.

"What would Iago do?"

Watching the following day above the orchards where Farmer Friendly had disappeared in his billowing truck, we witnessed great clouds of vultures or buzzards, descending in their immemorial gyres toward some hapless departed soul who lay somewhere disintact. Saying nothing both of us suspected it was our cat, god, who had perished perhaps at the vengeful hand of the farmer, or in the grip of a dog, perhaps Jingo.

Who knew?

In my mind's ear I fancied I heard the great beating of the birds' wings as they slung down toward their food. I fancied that their wings mimicked the sound of my beating heart. Flapping and flapping against the only long truth, each swung down and down.

I wondered if our spirits caused a similar sound as we prepared to be conceived, taxiing to the long truth, swinging down and down.

We decided to move on, knowing that we must give a call to Holy Hannah, as I called her, asking her to anticipate the possible arrival of god, should he appear. We had given him days to return, and he had not returned, and we feared the worst.

When Farmer Friendly was yet a long ways off we heard his chug-chuggings and we watched his filthy billowings. I could not decide if he drove a Ford or a Chevy, knowing the difference was as the difference between lemons and lemons, and knowing that both were brides of the oil boys.

He arrived and asked about Jingo, who was capably hiding. On querying, he said the birds were circling a cow that had tipped over. Clearly he wanted us to leave, so without any promptings we said we'd leave.

This news pleased the man, and from his cooler he produced some fresh meat and called it venison. Later I thought it tasted more like kangaroo. Meat is always welcome, whether landmeat or fish, and fish was plentifully circling in our gunnysack.

He climbed aboard his oilbeast and noised it up, climbing stern-first like any other old man would, and he waved and tipped his cowboy hat. Idly I wondered if his billowings presaged the truck, or followed it, and the wonder flicked away.

Idly as he drove away I watched the guns in the gunrack that was displayed in the truck's rear window, and my gaze flicked down to his bumpersticker, KILL 'EM ALL AND LET GOD SORT 'EM OUT. I wondered why people like him proclaimed it.

Another word, written in larger print, had preceded his bit of badinage, his warning, but I won't list what it was. It targetted whom he disfavored at the moment. Most targets are too easy to be fun, I thought.

It was later in the noon when I withdrew our submerged gunnysack from the water and found its twine had unraveled along the bottom seam, releasing our lunch and dinner back into the lake. Nothing had stayed, not even a crawdad.

I fancied Farmer Friendly carefully breathing through a reed while with nimble fingers he undid my labors, and then thought, equally idly, that he would probably have swiped the whole sack, fish and all. And it would have been only the simplest reciprocity, my mind parted.

So I cooked up a bit of the alleged venison, and we lunched.

Later, while Grit was committing poetry, or at least committing to paper something that at a glance looked suspiciously like the formidable fanciful feckless flotsamic stuff, I traipsed the area, looking for god. But cats are not easily found if they wish not to be found, and I admitted failure in a brief while.

Grit commented, when I returned, that in the morning it would be well to pack and leave, since our welcome had expired. He said, upon my asking, that his poem had been a failure, "beautiful in the immortal perception, and ugly in the temporal mind." I understood what he meant, or at least I understood what it would have meant had I uttered such an abstract statement, which is almost the same thing, I suppose.

Jingo ignored the disquisition wholly, which was a wise response for a dog, and he frolicked gaily in the lake, assuring us of catching no more fish. The dog had decided we were a family, inevitably. It occurred to me that perhaps we should have called him Iago, since he had displaced god, conscientiously.

The night was hung with clarity, boasting as if on black velvet an iridescent tiara of stars clustering a gorgeously pregnant moon exuding the mystery of mortality. I pictured the mortally immemorial umbilical chain that binds our living world maternally to the rock and the flame, from individual to individual to individual endlessly almost.

"Every imaginative individuated creature experiences occasions when the karma of past behavior is rinsed from our senses and we achieve an intimacy among the infinite, among the immortal substance which typically is beyond our reach as it is beyond our grasp.

"Our perceptions give us things of an absolute beauty which become because of our commonest activity blanched of truth, and become ugly to the temporal psyche. This is perhaps our cruellest inheritance from Eden, this dragging of the snake about our lives," Grit spoke directly to that portion of myself which perceived.

And of course the wonder passed.

Grit announced he had an especial treat, and in his

timely manner he displayed a tiny television that fed hungrily from our truck's battery.   Curiouser and curiouser, it accepted video tapes.

I wondered why he had brought along a bag of tapes, since I had assumed our journey was a length into the wilderness.   And now he played a tape of Chet Atkins doing concerts, with the camera playing along his intelligent honorable face, and his wizard's fingers.

That was a mesmerizing couple of hours.

And then came Jimmy Scott for an hour, exhaustingly.

First we went up, and then we went down.

And so to bed.

Early in the following morning I packed the truck, which was no very difficult task. Most of our gear had scarcely left the cargo bin, had just been stacked beside it. Some of Grit's favorites among his 20" x 30" framed photographs had been leaned against our neighboring trees or bushes, and his Theophile Steinlen favorite, TOURNEE DU CHAT NOIR, a drawing of a cat.

We had kept ourselves clean, thanks to the lake, and Grit had wearied of my joking too frequently that the reason we caught so many fish was because his bathing chummed the water. And our wee wardrobe was attiring the local bushes rather gracefully, augmenting their sartorial seasonal splendor, so it was easy to gather.

When Grit finally woke, and had washed, and had eaten remnants of the previous evening's venison, and potatoes, we rolled away. Playfully we asked the pooch Jingo if he wanted to accompany us, but the issue had been decided by the higher powers ages earlier. So our task was a mere compliance.

Mostly while we traveled we exchanged silences amicably, and it was commonly a good arrangement, but sometimes we decided, quite deliberately, to liven things up, and we told stories about our lives in those primeval days before we had wound our lives so inextricably into one communal pattern. Clearly, he had wanted familiness as much as I had wanted it, so when he adopted me it hadn't been wholly from altruism.

Nothing can be wholly from altruism, I figured.

"What of your life before, before we became us?" I nosed.

"What if I tell you of my early depredations, my dissolute and my wandering experience? Would that please your little animal curiosity? Would that appease you, and entertain you?" he asked.

I said it was a go.

"Twenty years ago I was approached by an Honduran editor to compose a centennial essay commemorating the birth of my favorite tenor, John Francis McCormack. I said what the hello, though I had not written an essay since school.

"I had a 2-week vacation coming up, so I arranged to take it at the wilderness cabin of some friends, in Potter Valley, California. I took with me everything I had that might be pertinent, and I was damningly sober.

"Every day I cogitated and I wrote, and bedtime was conscious, and was selfconsciously conscious. I did not feel piouser-than-thou, only stunned. And I worked well, completing a draft of 40 pages too ecstatically paced.

"Something clicked, and I found myself drinking in the evenings, and soon, after a pint or a fifth of tequila, I would drive into the town and would patronize the local saloon, fraternizing foolishly with the locals. When sober I promised I'd not do it again.

"When I sobered I felt embarrassed, each morning that arrived, and each morning I would promise not to suffer a repeat performance, playing the jackass. And each evening, after the loosening libations, I would play the jackass.

"So, I fixed one piece of my problem.

"The cabin was on the river, and had a long wide wild garden of gopher holes, blackberries, nettles, foxtails, bushes and trees. The garden bunched against 2 sides of the cabin, and was perhaps ¼ of an acre.

"Each evening, thereafter, as I embraced my very first drink, I'd walk onto the deck as the evening was darking into night, and I'd throw my keys out into the messy field, the unkempt garden, among the holes and the prickly plants. I had no flashlight.

"So therefore, every evening till I left, I'd drink and listen to the singing of John Francis McCormack. I permitted myself a suicide but not a murder, generously. Is that altruism?"

I didn't say much in response. That had been 20 years earlier, in an earlier existence, caught in an earlier war between his angels and his devils, other goods and other evils. He was better, though he was not good.

Wheels turned.

As our wheels pushed the previous earth behind us, and pulled toward us the earth of our futures, I pondered, idly I suppose, that Mr Grit had never been wafted a refreshing wind. If he'd found a wallet filled with money, he'd be more interested in the quality of the leather, and in owning the new-to-him wallet, than in spending the money it held.

His mind tended always to walk sideways.

The wheels turned.

Explain to me a wheel, and multiply it.

Moments happened, as they tend to, and he said, "What do you think?"

I said, "It seems a good waste of life, of consciousness."

He said, "Something must be given."

I said, "If a man is not strong enough to take."

He said, "Except for discourtesies, the gods are niggards."

I said, "We must make, if we do not find."

He considered, and he said, "Hrmwtz."

I said, in concession, "Hrmwtz." The sun was blue.

Innocence alone can find the wings to cry.

We arrived at a smallish town, and I parked the truck. Both Grit and I loved the treeishness of the town, situated in a sweet green valley, and we decided to live awhile in, among, and beside the town. Grit telephoned Holy Hannah concerning god, warning her to anticipate his not impossible arrival sometime in an unlooked-for future.

It may seem curious that we didn't discount the possibility of his returning to his old home, but cats do respond to place as mightily as dogs respond to family, and both Grit and I were astutely tardy drivers. We had no schedule and we observed no schedule, so we just poked along slow as molasses in January. Hurries are best ignored.

Dutifully we reconnoitered the perky little town, admiring the grace with which it enabled the lives of its residents, and we parked. Of course it had a plenty of town bums, which Grit called townbums, sprawling with an inegalitarian ease and sipping coffees. As many men have done, we wondered aloud which gods of the unbound prophet they worshipped, and what the dues were.

Grit made his phone call, concerning our absent feline, and we too coffee-ed, though he remarked, "Regardless of what Mr Dryden said, and his fellow eighteenth century dilettantes of the candled coffee houses, I seldom indulge in my fondness for coffee because it makes me stupid. Thinking fast is seldom thinking well. Speed introduces vacuity."

He commented that he might seek employment in the town, which had one small lumberyard, and a taxi stand. Both had small signs announcing job vacancies.

He walked into the local market, and we drove to the nearest rest stop, along the highway, and we boiled Yukon Gold potatoes, and we steamed a small fresh rabbit, with huge tofu chunks, fresh wheat germ, and pesto. Always I marvelled at the benison that was tofu, served hot as barbecued meat, and pesto.

We had seen a ramshackle shack in town, a little cabin of a house, and we wondered what its price was. It had a small yard, and a fig tree and a variety of persimmon trees. Fortunately it had no avocado tree. Avocadoes are dangerously tasty.

Duly we homed in as a family once more. We rented the cottage and we behaved flawlessly according to the established lights of the town. We took jobs at the local lumberyard, as father and son, so finally I acquired an accepted surname.

Many free days we spent basking in our yard, sitting, reading. Grit had always read desultorily, while my habit was to adhere to patterns I could distinguish, which faltered. He commented that my avowed insistence on patterns was only the bragging of a feigned omniscience, which was demonstrated when it faltered.

A vacuum surrounded us.

Both of us pondered his implications.

We laughed, a wee bit too loud.

"A joke," he said, "is a truth enclosed in civility. We laugh at the truth we perceive, and we laugh at our recognition of the civility which denies the truth. We bandy the shell, because it hides the kernal."

I said, "I'd love to see a meteorite fall, and land at our feet."

"Shut up," he explained.

While we labored in the days mostly we kept our own council, a behavioral irregularity which our fellows ascribed to an aloofness caused by our familial intimacy, I suspected. We were of course father and son, and sometimes that matters.

Mostly they resembled themselves just as they resembled those millions and squandered millions of other people who labor only to live. They chattered those vital meaninglessnesses, about sports and careers. They wore jewelry in and on their bodies, and used perfumes the men called cologne. They tattooed themselves, and each tattooed the other, and they paid strangers money to tattoo their hides with temporarily brightly colored cartoons and slogans.

They smoked tobacco, and marijuana, crack cocaine and hashish. They ate white bread and greasy salty burgers. They joked about people whom they considered genetically reproachable. They envied the rich and hated the poor, relatively speaking.

In their innocence as innocent as kittens and potentially as destructive, extroverts are materialists. If materialism is the great honorable activity, why doesn't it attract the finest people in the world? Why do the finest shy from it? I wondered.

Thought is the great bugaboo, and extroverts

vacuum their minds with empty cacophonies to be free from thought's intrusion. Noises out-shouted thoughts, noises from television, from radio, from dealings. Noising seduced them.

I liked these people, and they saddened me.

What, I asked, is honor? The self, abjuring its ego?

I liked them.

Unless you happen to be a flea injudiciously perched upon a dessicated nose within a closely seamed stone sarcophagous inside a mausoleum in the local churchyard, it is difficult not to become an active participant in the life of a town if you chance to live in that town. We were not grotesquely reclusive in our new surroundings, our new town.

We did our very best to be friendly with almost everybody, and we shopped for groceries, and for a bit of gas, and for raiment. We chatted comfortably with almost everybody, learning slowly the new language, ever attentive to signals.

And we pooled our fledgling understandings.

The postmaster was a thoughtful old fellow, considering himself to be an historian and a geographer because he had seen and handled so many stamps, and knew names. His heart was unhappy, because like Falstaff he was fat as butter. He put up signs in his post office, in which he spelled material as materiel, and he felt wise whenever anybody tried to correct him: Grit commented that after the fellow's initial misspelling of the word he had looked it up and discovered his error had been indicative of an intuitive genius, "And if the fool would persist in his folly he would become wise."

Mrs Postmaster recognized the inevitable, she being one of those folks who loved to read the obituaries in the paper, and her eye was already upon possible future soulmates. Mortgages are immortal. Death is always retail to those people who bother with it, and her eye was on the dollar. She wasn't about to squander her real kindnesses on the undeserving.

Mr P liked to chat with us, and Mrs P was always inviting Grit to come in through the back door when Mr P was away. Something she had seen in his demeanor intrigued her, I reckoned, despite appearances.

"Beware her day of reckoning," I cautioned him.

"I thank you for disobeying our injunction," he murmured.

Mrs Postmaster was younger by far than was Mr Postmaster, which might have explained just why she married him. It had certainly been for her an act of condescension, since, as every woman does, she had married spectacularly beneath herself.

Sometimes he would sneak around to our kitchen door, rather in the late of night, and he would sneak a soda. For him that was violent rebellion, we supposed. He would throw the thing down his hatch, and would rush back to her to be meek forever again, till next time.

One black night after he had scuttled off, I suggested to Grit, that it might be a kindness to slip in some potassium cyanide, next time. Grit's shoulders drooped, and the axis of his mouth drooped, and he said, "Eleemosynary gestures are so expensive, alas. Sympathy is so much easier to bear than is empathy, the sympathetic than the empathic.

"The gods of this world are pale hungry bitches," he concluded, and he turned away.

Intimacy is vital to our healthy, happy development as individuals and as a species, and as an earthborne culture, and it became apparent to my admittedly partisan observations that my continued presence was as beneficial to Grit as his presence was to me. His had been a trial by loneliness for years and for years, for a lifetime, and he had felt genetically forsaken, desperate. His sometime response had been to descend into his preternatural glooms, sometimes drunkenly.

I had never seen him drunk.

Suicide tugged at his sleeves, imploring, promising Valhalla.

And now he was balancing, conscientiously. And in every town there are people who see.

He held to me, and he held to his job. His eye was expanding about the town, holding the town like an oyster holds an irritating bit of grit. His eye held each individual and measured that individual, discovering patterns where they existed. He realized that cities held a superior anonymity to towns, and yet perhaps he had experienced enough of anonymity. Perhaps now he wanted to participate, if participation were possible for such as he.

Dilemma.

Our new town had 2 markets, a small and upscale, and a larger and plainer. The littler market boasted 51 brands of mustard, 93 brands of olive oil, 75 varieties of nut butter, 100 of breads.

Commonly we chose the supermarket, the larger and the plainer, except when our taste was exact. One day alone in the check-out line Grit was caught peeking by the checker, who suddenly shone smiles. From then on, for a long while we had either to avoid her line or her store.

"Peeking must be a matter for the nicest discretion," I reminded him.

He grunted unamiably.

"Although   everybody   does   it,"   I   suggested

generously.

He grunted unamiablier, scowling at my trespass.

"Maybe you should ask her out," I suggested helpfully.

He shook his head in mock despondency, and I fancied I heard a sound like melting ice slopping around in a cooler. I did not grin.

OUR TOWN was just what Thornton Wilder described when he wrote his famous story. When you are with your cronies you refer to OUR TOWN, which is also your town, and it is everybody's town. This is of course inevitable, and it is rightly so.

Our town had its complement of oddball critters.

A critter of course is a creature, somebody who was created by a creator, by a creative. Everybody who was created is a critter, even if the creator wears a dark hat and lives in the shadows.

We had a 70 year old boy who transmogrified toilet seats into effectual guitars which were purchased generously by rock stars. He looked like a boy and acted boyishly, lacking only a propeller-driven beanie, and a slingshot in his jeans, to complete the picture. His skin was translucent, like a victim's of multiple strokes.

We had homeless people, whose lives were as sweet as rancid cream. I decline to tell you the stories that would curdle your dreams.

We had a man, hairy as a furball, who walked backward.

We had our allotted gamut.

Miss Emily Dickinson referred to morticians as belonging to the appalling trade, and our mortician, our undertaker, was called Adam Sherbet. Almost I suspected that during his own autopsy it would be revealed that his blood was copper-based, green as the lights of envy. He presented himself as a dapper version of Peter Lorre, circa 1930, always youngish.

Our bookshop belonged to Mary, a lady brave and foolish enough even to stock this book you hold in your hands. Those people who saw her customers tended to look at one another knowingly, to tap their brows with the tips of their forefingers, and to shake their heads slowly, feelingly. It was called, SECRET PASSAGES.

> Mary has a bookshop
> but folks begrudge buying:
> betraying their television's
> worse to them than dying.

> Mary has a bookshop
> and advertises brains
> to those dot-commie predators
> who keep our world in chains.

> Mary has a bookshop
> whose volumes seldom sell:
> a reprimanded audience
> just wishes books in hell.

> Mary has a bookshop
> she built to salve the soul
> but virtual morality
> is everybody's goal.

Our minds do love to invent reasons to misbehave, I thought.

OUR TOWN had also a trickling of schoolteachers, captive sociologists, I thought. Like the fire brigade and the police brigade, mostly they were decent people

bulwarking against chaos and brutishness, I thought. I
admired healers, I thought.

Everybody of course was trying to score.

Mr Postmaster had never been well, I suspected.
Every morning he fried a pound of bacon, and fried half
a dozen eggs in the bacon soup, and ate the mass in a
mouth swilling with sugary coffee. His distrust of
vegetables was legendary in the town.

His lunch consisted of a family-sized pepperoni pizza
with extra cheese, which he ate with a mouth bubbling
with cola. His face was red enough to stampede a bull,
and frothed like a cauldron of boiling bloody grease.
When friends complained about his health, and his
rubicund appearance, he shrugged and joked.

And so he died in bed.

Flags drooped, because everybody loved him.

He'd been a church-going man when it was
convenient, so they had a church-going funeral, and he
was tucked into the churchyard in back, with a little
written tablet of stone marking the spot.

Every funeral should be raining softly.

Darkly dressed, we stood in the sun.

"He has ceased to manufacture his past," said he.

"Is that all?" said I.

"If God, whose dwelling is the infinite NOW, ceases to
participate in the manufacture of His past, which too is
ours, then everything has never been," he said, "since
past is all."

"But this man was not God. He was only the
lookingglass for everything according to his eyes," I said.

"I can only examine the lookingglass," said he.

"I choose not to whine," said I.

"Me too, sometimes," he said.

Did we lie. The sun was flailing softly, and I watched

idly the shapes emerging from the scudding clouds and disappearing again into themselves. The clouds looked as if they had been stirred by a finger.

The sun flung its arm across its face and we shivered.

After the funeral and its funereal solemnities, we had no crazy irish wake with kegs and quarts of ales and whiskies, or whiskey, but rather an atmosphere of communal quiet pressed down upon everybody as if an invisible fog had settled in. It was a time for reflection, for remembrance.

Grit and I walked languidly toward our home, to our cottage in its tiny valley which was dropped within a bigger valley and which was columned round by proud vertical pilings of ancient redwood trees.

I said, "During our time almost never have you volunteered advice, although subsequent or consequent events have proven that I had needed that advice, and sorely. Why is this?

"I have seldom hesitated to offer you my best advice, though you have not asked for it. We seem to lack reciprocity, parity," I said.

Both of us were quiet for a moment, and it occurred to me that when we think aloud our listener must often suspect of us complaining, while in fact we are only arranging informations in our mind. I did not suspect that Grit would misunderstand me, since I had never known him to misunderstand me accidentally. When he misunderstood me it was invariably intentional.

He said, "I lack the benefit of your inexperience. Ponder this response for a year and ask me again. I will be waiting," and I knew that he would be waiting. It was enough.

As we duly ascended those few steps that led to our door, he paused, considering something he understood to be important. He faced me squarely, so our forms became parallel. He lifted his forearms extending his fingertips, and I reciprocated.

So we two stood face to face as a single form, held fingertips to fingertips.

He said, "Years ago I was informed that advice is only criticism, and that criticism presupposes omniscience and a recognition of one's personal infallibility, a state we might call perfection. My tres generous informant then advised me: NEVER CRITICIZE YOUR FRIEND.

"It can prove a bleak and hallowed experience for us to contain our individual poisons, and it is my effort."

Gently he rebuffed me, and our fingertips fell like light snowflakes down and also down. "Is that sufficient," he said, though he was almost asking.

"Yes," I said. "Am grateful. Helps," I murmured. Did.

As I slept that night I visited a house inhabited by my mother and my father. Shadows hung upon the whole house, the whole neighborhood, and his voice mocked her boomingly and she sought me frantically.

A barge-sized debris box was in the parkingspaces in the brief driveway, and I hid behind the big box smoking a big havana, plentiful traces from its smoke wafting into and through the house, which too was almost as dark as night. I could feel the existence of other people in the house, clustering the walls, shadowy. Siblings, perhaps?

She was querulous, frightened, anxious that I was not apparent, anxious that I might be hiding from her, from them. His mocking voice challenged her, deriding her insecurities, inflaming them. They preyed upon her like locusts preying upon fields of grain.

Her ragged face spoke through the shadowy doorway,

seeking me, and I held back, hiding. Like columns of artillery, tears moved down her face, and in the scant light it shone.

He was only a voice, bouncing loud.

Our cottage had an excellent floor plan for any healthy small family. It had a livingroom, a biggish kitchen, a dining nook, a thoroughly adequate bathroom, a largish bedroom and a smallish bedroom, and a tiny bathroom. It had a garage, and a lovely backyard with fruit trees, and a wee creek sputtered or cooed beside it.

Of course Grit had the largish bedroom, and I had the smallish bedroom. Each bedroom had a bed, dresser, closet, and a comfy chair nicely stuffed.

Our policy was that all doors were to remain open except when privacy was required. "Personalities close when the doors close," Grit had said, accepting that occurrences in bathrooms and sometimes in bedrooms required closings.

Often he read on his bed, with his door open, and so did I. Often one of us was in the bedroom and the other in the livingroom, or both of us would be in his appropriate bedroom. Pressure was nil.

This evening, after we returned from Mr Postmaster's funeral, Grit retired into his bedroom, with his door open, and read stretched on his bed, lying on his back, or lying on a side facing his lamp. I dawdled, playing on the television, and then dawdled, playing with Jingo, and then I walked to Grit's door, knocked softly and without waiting for any response I walked in and I sat in his chair.

When it was convenient, he set his book aside, focussed on me, and inquired, "Huh?" It was a friendly lazy grunt.

I said, "What really is a funeral?"

He said, "Yes," and he paused. His eyes accepted a certain amount of light that in the room floated against the walls, floor, and ceiling, but the light was an irrelevancy to his contemplations. His thinkings opened further doors somewhere I could not see, and some portion of his psyche was reaching through those doors and walking those further corridors.

He said, "A funeral is like a person's name. It is an affirmation that civility will continue uninterruptedly, and civilly almost disregards whomever it appears most to concern. It reaffirms the covenant we as responsible gregarious beings must adhere to, regardless of our preferences. It announces that nothing in our general passage has changed though we are lamentably fewer.

"Yes we cry, although crying must be a private thing to be achieved genuinely. Our profoundest goodbyes must be spoken privately to be achieved genuinely. In that profoundest internal keep that is the self we must observe further obeisances if genuineness of utterance is to occur, and if we are to accomplish what our individual humanity requires.

"A funeral is but wind, as is the air we breathe, the atmosphere in which we have our being. It prepares us for something more difficult, something essential to our wholeness." Every word had been spoken with an increasing slowness, and he was done, he wondered.

He looked the question at me, and I said, "Yes," and I walked away. The dog and I chatted awhile, and then came the bed.

Our rather odd journey had begun on the coast, taken us inland among the flatlanders, desert-dwellers, and lake-dwellers, and had returned us to the coast albeit onto a more northerly spot. Grit distrusted those who dwelt too far from the life-according oceans, and I of course without the least demur acceded to his whims. I had neither thoughts nor feeling about such things.

My urgent desire was not to be urban. City is poison, and prison, and poison.

The funeral came and went, as funerals do, and after a bit we had a day alone. Neither of us felt an urgency either toward or away from any particular activity, so we decided to walk through the surrounding trees, staying on the roads and pathways mostly. Jingo was decidedly for the romp, and leapt about.

We passed a little homestead where chickens were bred and harvested, and a small sign advertized eggs, meat, and chicks. We watched the hens pecking, and roosters running about with their hands in their pockets. And there were a few ducks.

Grit told me, parenthetically, that it was customary for drakes to rape hens. "Miscegenation at its best," I responded glibly.

"Ponder it a bit more," he upbraided mildly.

"Explain," I requested.

"With just that dismissive attitude every technologically superior animal treats every technologically inferior animal it encounters, and the resultant turmoil is a reassertion of primal chaos. And the behavior of every tribal society is only an extrapolation of individual behaviors, denied by the individuals, commonly. And there's the rub," he said.

Of course I felt smalled.

"And then," I commented wisely, "A bobcat struts through the yard and cops the lot."

"The tiniest, perfectly coordinated untameable feline, with a truncated tail and a face like a crawdad's, invisible as cancer's bent. And then," he paused, "the farmer does or does not shoot the kitty."

We walked on past, showing the scene occasionally to one another, or introspecting. Shadows hung like brown banners among the trees, and like time's weavers we threaded among them.

Jingo ran and barked, performing dog's inalienable duty doggily. He missed several trees with his dutiful spout, but only several. Often he'd glance back to ascertain that he still led us, and to smile.

I mentioned to Grit that Jingo appeared to confuse consequence with subsequence, and he only laughed lightly, commenting, "I think that's a generous assessment of our condition, also. Indeed, always I've suspected that I would rather be a follower than a leader, but I haven't discovered anybody I wanted to follow, or anybody I wanted to lead. It is not however a very pressing dilemma."

"Didn't Mr Shakespeare warn us about that?" I asked, a shade too cutely.

"What did he say?"

"Neither a follower nor a leader be," I said and smiled almost sickly, smarmily almost, smugly certainly. Grit groaned, muttering that I was at best an unscrupulous pickpocket of lint and small coins.

"Sorry," I claimed.

I knew he was my leader, or that he was one of my leaders, and yet I was unconcerned by what he had said. He hadn't been referring to him and me, to our relationship, which was an almost barbless relationship.

Yes.

No sane intelligent honorable man enjoys rehashing the old plots of his laborious money-makings, especially on his weekends or his vacations, but I was bold and enjoyed the rights of intimacy, I thought. So it was that as we casually sauntered along the pathways just thinking irregularly, haphazardly, I said, "Tell me a curiosity or a drollery reminiscent of your years and earlier years in laborings."

He replied, "Some several years ago I loaded a customer's pickup truck with what lumber he required and had paid for, and I watched as from his truck's toolbox he whipped forth a longish rope constructed of a multitude of silk neckties linked from end to end.

"Using this odd contrivance he then fastened his purchase to his truck's lumber-racks. I knew just enough about silk italian neckties to fix their prices from $60 to $200. I asked for his explanation.

"He said that every Christmas and Easter, every birthday and every anniversary, and at other times throughout every year in remembrance, his mother presented him with a silk italian necktie, and finally he had discovered a use for the things.

"He laughed and scoffed and he asked me what I thought of it all. My only reply was that I wished I had a mom. That did deflate his hilarity, just a bit, I noticed," Grit reminisced.

His punchline did ruin the drollery, I thought.

He said, after we had strolled awhile through the fringes of grass that bordered our trail, "Tell me one."

I pondered, and told him that it had happened years ago while I was delivering booze and tobacco for the saloon. I said my particular assignment during one particular evening was to deliver booze and tobacco to one of our regular customers who lived in a trailer park, and when I arrived, a trifle too disingenuously I said, "Hi, Jerry. What's the matter with you? You look like you've been rode hard and put away wet."

Jerry had replied, I said, that the previous day had been exceedingly difficult, and that when he had arrived home in the afternoon, all he had wanted to do, "was to drink myself to Bolivia."

I responded, I said, "I am told La Paz is nice this time of year."

And Jerry said, "What the hell you talking about?"

Duly, Grit laughed in his customary silent manner and silently slapped air near his legs with his hands. Sometimes he guffawed, and sometimes he laughed silently using every appropriate thespian gesture except for the gesture of sound. I liked them both, as gestures.

We continued our march desultorily, saunteringly, our pathway being buffetted by each passing fancy. We watched the shadows as they invested the near sky and the far, the near earth and the farther, watching the grays, the browns, the greens and the fugitive whites. Eventually my wits broke through the flummox and I asked, for I could bear the suspense no longer, "Why did you permit yourself to fall into a knowledge of silk italian neckties?

"I have never seen you wear a tie, except on that one occasion," I furthered.

"It was to satisfy a passing need, as most knowledge is," he responded. "I no longer possess the knowledge or its understanding, although perhaps if circumstances demanded my response the knowledge and its understanding might reassert themselves. That happens, too," he said.

"We are malleable mutts, and not to be ashamed of it. It is how we mark our territories, an assertion of pretense. When we bend it cannily it serves us well, for our nonce," he said, and Jingo came strolling by with a squirrel in his chops, proud as a cool bright summer's day.

"See that?" he murmured happily, placidly. The

squirrel was playing dead, rather too well, I thought. But Grit gently lifted the squirrel from Jingo's grip and deftly tucked it behind his back as he counterfeited a motion of throwing it for the dog, who ran instantly into the game.

Grit set the squirrel behind a tree, and it twitched and ran a tree away and up into the canopy of trees. Jingo bounded back to us and I threw a small branch for him and he darted off after it yelping with glee.

I said, "Tell me about your father."

He paused, and said, "It's a fair question, admittedly. What is there to tell. I have watched you studying those men we work for. My father was like them, only exaggeratedly. It is the old story. Maybe he was your father's identical brother.

"ECCE HOMO. He was a shadow caught by the sun.

"He was the shiniest average and hated that word. He was a cretin who valued above all non-things his selfishness. His favorite arrow in his quiver was the arrow the color of perpetual ignorance.

"Always he had something he was hiding, that was not unique. He was rattled when he suspected his hidden thing existed, yet he demanded to conceal it anyway.

"About women he snickered like a boy, scoffed at men. His lips bubbled with contempt toward anybody who quested. He relished that ultimate privilege of being him: the man. Ecce homo.

"His mind slammed shut but somehow little whispers of light slipped through, disturbing rules.

"He was like ourselves. Every comprehensive man experiences those failures in his being. It is the dues. It too is our inheritance from Eden," he said.

"The old sun is quenching," he said.

"The size of a man is the size of his failures," he said.

I said, "Tell me about your mother."

He said, "That's briefer.   She wanted to be my father's wife only, so she strove to become his mirror, a flattering mirror such as monarch's use.

"Deliberately she incited his smalling tendencies believing it would provoke an adhesion. Of course it could not.

"Without its reflection a being continues, but deprived of its object a mirrored response unexists. His response was not adhesion, but contempt. He hated the mirror for exhibiting an imperfect likeness.

"She never understood the illimitations of abandonment, poor thing, nor that she had engendered them.

"I could weep," he concluded, and his tone conveyed conclusion.

My promptings were through.

Somewhat better, I thought, I understood my predicament.

Sometimes understanding is better.

Every trail must end where it begins, and our saunter having achieved its middling limit we began our trek back to our cottage. When we were in the appropriate area I glanced about surreptitiously hoping to find our squirrel waving his gratitude toward us from the green canopy, but he wasn't available for such a gesture.

Jingo stopped frequently to roll in things I choose not to ponder, and to eat similar delicacies. Dogs are animals, I thought with a quivering lip, and cringed.

Our passing feet scuffed the leaves as we approached our house, and we were alone among all we could reach. Night was closing and a light was from our windows because we had left it on as a beacon.

I said, "You have been my father and my brother and

my friend. It is important that you hear my thanks. I would jump into the dark for you."

He said, "Sons and father, wives and husbands, lovers, always betray whom they should not. We are brothers and friends and somehow circumstances will betray us. Gladly we must repay debts that should have belonged to other people.

"Though the good sun walk
across the fields of the sky
yet we will be friends.

"Because these things are so exquisitely difficult to speak of, it is important and it is vital that we do speak them. It is humanly almost impossible truly to be friends rather than to be merely temporary accomplices, so it is good to try and to try and to try.

"The pleasure is in the unrepentant difficulty," he said.

He lifted his hand and he cupped it behind my nape and held it against my neck there as the dark was closing still. In our focus the light from our home beckoned continuedly and we joined it in the house and we were glad.

"Arably responds
earth to formulaic sun
welcoming harvest," I said, but I said it in my personal silence and it was unlisted.

The time was good.

As we entered our cottage our answering machine's light called out to us and Grit's finger brushed its button, and the voice of the widow, formerly Mrs Postmaster, invited Grit to visit her anytime he found the trip convenient. She invited him to use either her livingroom doorway or her kitchen doorway, "the neighbors be damned. Whatever tickles your fancy."

We were in stasis, his back to me, and I said, "Maybe you should boogie on over and award her your treasure."

Without turning, he said, "Such speech is not becoming, my friend. Dulce et decorum est: it is natural and healthy that women and men should entertain one another. As an expression of kindliness it costs a woman nothing to entertain a man, and costs him nothing to reciprocate.

"But I will not go because the woman is bereft of kindliness. Her desire to gain some measure of an ascendancy she believes to exist, causes her to be clenched with selfishness despite her protesting smiles. Such a behavior is as dishonorable as was that little unconsidered trifle which slipped from your lips a moment ago," he said, his back still to me, and he proceeded to our rooms.

I stood in alabaster embarrassment. He paused in his stridings, turned to face me, and he smiled. The man was incapable of rancor, and I felt blessed.

Duly I must confess that even while merely a whippersnapper I had in my regions a nest of demons who could not leave a good thing unchallenged. I knew he was an angel to me, permissive and forgiving of my youthful follies, and yet I challenged his supremacy with a childish cavil.

I said, "It is true that through my mind an unclean tinkling briefly flashed, and yet the whole burden of my quip's malevolence was briefer than a cosmic ounce and sooner than a cosmic inch. Almost, I was only entertaining."

He faced me now and I faced by him as I walked to the bathroom, and I said, "If you need me I'll be making you a party hat." He was paused and he held his pause, and I closed the bathroom door behind me.

Age is irritating.

Our livingroom had no carpet but did have an old de-threading rug that was uncoiling like a snake, and on that old rug our dog Jingo spent much of his time, gnawing on things, himself included. A joint of bone had come under his scrutiny, and under his jaws' grip, and this night he worried it, trying to get some blood from it, gnawing this way and then gnawing that way, ascertaining that no portion of it wasn't drenched with slobbering dog-spit. This pleased him, and I was affable enough, though it was my wrist he gnawed on.

The telephone rang, and customarily I answered it. Holy Hannah was on, announcing that our cat, god, had arrived at our old apartment and that she had corraled the critter and held him for us.

I told Grit and he said okay, and I told her okay, and I hung up. He came sauntering in, and said, okay. I said okay and he said okay. He scratched his whiskers and then scratched and picked his belly, and he grunted amiably, said okay, and he walked back into his bedroom.

A few minutes later he said okay.

I replied okay in a lowered voice, just to be pleasant.

Early in the dark morning the rains began and soaked the earth and the trees and every house. Every creature was approached closely by the seething wet seeping everywhere.

When the sky lightened the rains continued wetting everything, and finally the sun walked across the ceiling of the sky like a wet spider hiding, not yet waiting.

Almost suddenly, not quite suddenly, the clouds retreated and the sun jumped into everybody's eyes, and all across the town we watched a blizzard of termites winging. They filled the roadways and the houses, and clouded every tree.

In every stream and lake the fish were busy lipping them.

The people stood and watched, and gaped.

We knew our god was safe with Holy Hannah, till this next week-end at the least, so we continued our work-week undisturbedly. In the evenings after a leisurely dinner he in his room and I in my room would read copies of the same book, John Murray's 1928 edition of Arthur Conan Doyle's SHERLOCK HOLMES. Grit kept saying it had the most delicious atmosphere in all of literature. He said, "for the literary fly-on-the-wall, the voyeur of the salon, it can't be surpassed. Like that scribblers' insect we watch our earlier fellows at their table and at their toils, and they become as if our heroes.

"Some folks compare Holmes to our christian savior, Jesus of Nazareth, Christ, who had a clique by whom he was variously worshipped, tolerated, and betrayed, and who was consequently martyred, revivified, and translated. Holmes had effectually the identical clique, functionally," he said.

"Other folks criticize his table manners, and comment curiously concerning his toilet manners: did his hand go around or through? did he pick his nose? did he cough blood? was his anemia persistent?

"Once again he is famouser than is Charlie Chaplin's little tramp, and is almost family in our reflections. Because of him I wonder, and I laugh, and though his pain may have been profound for him it is never profound for me except if I pretend it to be, and so is qualified luxuriously," he said.

"Because of him I laugh," he said.

I said I understood, and sometimes I think I understood.

We may agree in friendliness, though not in actuality, without lying, I thought. And the actuality might come with sufficient pondering, and I was willing to try, I thought. Gambits are necessary for functioning, I thought.

It has been often commented upon that weekends do arrive whether we are prepared for them or not, and whether we wish them to arrive or not. And this following weekend did opportunely arrive, as we had expected it to arrive, and we woke in the morning with our truck packed sufficiently for a jaunt on the road.

When we had left the seaside city we had headed inland, but somehow had wended back to the coast just miles and many miles farther north. Our truck was a divining rod and we were dowsers, and the waters couldn't keep us away, I guess.

But now our journey had a definite aim, which was to reach again into the colossal building we had lived in, with its lofts and its apartments and its little meretricious shops fronting on the streets, and to get our long lost cat, god.

We drove for hours and hours, and for hours. Grit almost never drove past 40 miles per hour, and being his psychic sidekick I complied with his desires on the matter. Still, the swollen earth rolled under our rolling rubber feet, and slowly we arrived.

"Well," Holy Hannah commented, inappropriately, I thought, "if it ain't pieces of Tweedledum and Tweedledee. Howdy, boys. What's the pickin's?"

Clearly she was a bit miffed by our recent reticence, and perhaps we should have picked up our cat sooner, according to her wishes. Who knew? I wasn't too concerned, and Grit was busy communicating with her very much nonverbally, with facial slides and winks and intonations. I was grateful for the exclusion.

That night with my scrawny little god I slept on her couch, and he purred fitfully on my belly, sometimes stabbing a claw into my nipple or clambering over alongside the back of my noggin to lick the salt from my ear's underhangs. When I could tolerate his abradings no longer I snuck in to the more public of her 2 bathrooms and showered lengthily, regardless of proprieties concerning her towels and soaps.

In the morning, and during the day, and toward the evening, we dutifully returned to OUR TOWN. God and Jingo must be reconciled, somehow, and I was prepared for the struggle.

Still we drove at 40, ignoring the tributes folks fingered and honked at us as they scrupulously passed us on the road. Speedy lives lead nowhere, I thought, just like ours.

In this morning when we began our journey again toward OUR TOWN our god was again in an exceedingly sturdy cat-carrier in the cargo bin of the befallen pickup truck, a belt wrapped around the belly of the box, and a widely woven hempen net across the box, and across the boxes and bags of books and of videos and of similar pelf we had reacquired.

Our family god had once resembled a beautifully albeit grotesquely enlarged mouse, or a furry fat buddha, and now resembled a shrunken mole-rat or some haggard bedraggled eremite who had just barely escaped to his mountainous cell before he was tortured into martyrdom by the town's respectable folks in some feudal century of holy spectacle.

We assumed that most of his travelling had occurred

at night, when dogs and birds and people could be avoided, and he had been starved and torn. His ears resembled birds-of-paradise, shapely misshapen effusions remnantly scabby.

I thought it wise to be wary of god, and I was wise. Upon our arrival at home I carried him in his carrying-box into my bedroom which was a trap prepared. My door I closed, leaving as his only exit an inch of draft below my fastened window. That inch was always there.

His litterbox was prepared, with a fresh plot of sand. His bowls were prepared, one with water, and his kibbled food I poured into another bowl, and his canned food I spooned into a third.

The trepid cat prowled.

His careful eye measured that inch of draft. He investigated under the bed, and checked the closet for intruders, etc. He sniffed the pooper, and he dipped finger into the water. He smelt his food by listening as he strutted by.

He pounced onto the pile of clean sand and squirmingly rolled and bounced. He twisted onto his back and he paddled about on its waves, and he leapt upright. He stepped out gingerly, and daintily shook each foot individually.

He strutted perhaps a yard away and he turned and returned to and into the necessary sandbox. Carefully he stepped backward until his fanny touched the sandbox wall, and he ejected his torpedo over the wall of the box and it landed on my bedroom rug.

And so I was instructed to use a taller box. And so I learned to spread the newspaper's business section beneath the box. Sometimes I used the society section.

I understood it would require a month to orient him, till his 2 delicately cunning ends forgot to read the magnets in the wind, till this house was his home.

Grit asked, "Where did you learn about controlling the window?"

I repled, "When I lived with my presumptive mother and father I fed feral cats, or strays, in a basement room which had a window opening from the side. I fastened its maximum aperture at approx 3 inches, maybe 3½, using a dowel.

"One day I heard a screaming and I descended to discover that my most recently attended rescuee had tried to squeeze his body vertically through the aperture. One outside of his ribcage had conveniently collapsed sufficiently to allow his progress, but when the windowstile moved into his solar plexus, the gap between his rib-sides, it expanded again and he was trapped inextricably.

"It was a bitch to release him. Without breaking his ribs, I mean, which would have foiled the point of the maneuver. What is the purpose of rescuing something only to destroy it?"

Grit said, "Did your ostensible mother and father approve of your rescuing those misfortunate felines?"

I said, "They said cats can't plow."

"My mother and my father," I said, "appeared as innocent as cherries freshly plucked from the vine. Unfortunately, cherries do not grow on the vine either."

He said, "Your homiletic parenthesis makes no sense."

I said, "I know, but I'm fond of it. I've been arranging it for days, for just such an occasion, and now, like an ugly baby, I've delivered it. So now, like an ugly baby, I can forget it."

"Yikes," he said, with calm revulsion.

"I know," I said.

Apparent sound.

It is almost never easy to be reborn, and sometimes the earlier's birth will reassert itself briefly. Grit felt so thunderously wealthy with self he popped into a saloon, sat at a table, and gaped when asked for his choice. He gulped, said, "Tea, please," and was brought some.

He listened. One fellow bibber asked a fellow bibber, "Tell us what words Alice found," ignoring Grit.

"Napoleon Bonaparte," the fellow began, "was tactician and strategist. Simultaneously, almost, he evaluated arrays of sequential moves, each sequence in the total pattern, and there were palimpsests of total patterns, in this context, possessing one established first move followed by its necessary second move followed by its necessary third, vaguely ad finitum.

"His broad mind held a hundred sequences, or a thousand, approximately, in this context, and they in motion shimmering.

"As he evaluated he listed first his favorite first followed by his favorite second followed by his favorite third followed by his favorite fourth, et cetera. Then he listed his second favorite first followed by his second

favorite second followed by his second favorite third
followed by his second favorite fourth etc. Then his
third favorites, sequentially, and then his fourth
favorites etc.

"Epiphanies are a bitch," the fellow maximmed, "and
he epiphanied. And he listed each minor sequence a
second time, and he rearranged his mind and he listed
each minor sequence a third. Then he placed his first
second third, fourth, and his fourth third second first.

"Shall we discuss stipulative punctilio?"

Grit tucked in his pinkie, and Grit strode, done. His
voice advised his inhabitant selves, "The burly worm et
the bird, brothers."

"She died so hard and fast she rang for an hour."

In the morning while breakfasting we noticed our answering-machine's light was blinking once again. It was customary that our telephone's ringer was silenced completely, so we were not surprised that we had not heard its clickings.

Holy Hannah was on the line again. She said initially that her brief message was for me, not for Grit. She said she had enjoyed our visit and that I was growing leggily, and that our domestic arrangement was clearly doing both of us good, making us well. She said it was very important that I keep Grit on the straight and narrow path toward righteousness, for it was only when he was on that difficult path that he was able to permit himself any measure of happiness. She said that it displeased her to inform me that my mother had died.

I closed the connection.

Grit extended his hand and I took it, gave him a manly handshake and a brave smile. I released his hand. I phoned our employer and asked if I might take the day off.

I took Jingo to the quiet beach, which was rolling growlingly. He ran and ran and swam and swam. The day was misty, foggy. The impenetrable high mist extended to the hypothetical end of the infinite horizon. Jingo ran I'd guess 4 miles into the horizontal surf. I saw kayakers, 2 kayakers, paddling together almost at the line of vision, and heard them across the foggy reach talking to Jingo as his head swam by them.

Jingo'd never had such fun in his life.

The sun had turned its back on us, and mist floated down and wet my clothing. Jingo appeared out of nowhere and flung his sea across my face and my clothing. I fended his sea with my arm, across my face.

That day the sea was wet, and I was wet. Jingo was wet.

It was not a bad day.

My poor head was a deserted slaughterhouse.

My brain was the space between hammer and anvil.

In all that day I had no mind. I had only the envelope containing mind. My mind was blank as the weariest rock, slick as silica, salt dry. I watched the day and I watched through the day the night enveloping day.

"What is MOTHER, a mother, the desperate and obliging current of motheringness? What is the quintessence of mothering? What is MOTHER? Is a mother the envelope containing day?" I wondered.

"From what broad ocean come the green bubbles of the spring?"

I was grateful she had never loved me.

Jingo's paws were filthy with the clean sea as he laid them upon my chest, and with his wet rag of a tongue he slapped my face. With my hands I framed his face tightly and I spoke those foolish words dogs need.

Home was calling.

Early in the evening Jingo and I arrived home, and Grit suggested that he and I take in a burrito and a movie. Because of our relative poverty, and because of our contemplative preferences, we went out very seldom, and his suggestion was welcomed enthusiastically.

It has often been suggested that most interesting people are moneyless, and though we were certainly rather moneyless I doubt we were very interesting. Grit was certainly an articulate fellow, but most of my cogitable ploddings were not articulable, at least for me. Movies typically are too sparely contemplable to be entertaining, and so most of our evenings were a tad bookish.

This evening was to see Carlos Saura's GOYA IN BORDEAUX, and as we wended toward it we were stopped by our village's preacher, priest, or pastor, whatever he was. He had heard of my mother's passing, and assumed she had been Grit's erstwhile wife, and he wanted to vent his professional sympathy. Towns talk.

I consider myself a connoisseur of hands, and immediately upon extracting my hand from his I wiped my hand surreptitiously on the seat of my trousers. Shaking hands with him was like being grabbed by a gigantic marshmallow that had been soaking in the cold acidic soup of an out-house toilet all during a long dark winter's night.

He commented that my mother's death probably made me jittery with unspecified anticipations, with frightening presentiments, and he grinned at me with an omniscient benevolence, being God's chosen confidence-man. But he was describing blood on invisible hills, since actually I felt as calm as if I'd been killed yesterday. I felt a devastating emptiness, and that was everything.

Finally, and with a resolute civility, we escaped the clacking mechanical clutches of Writ's interpreter, and we proceeded toward the movie. In a faultlessly timely manner I had affected incomprehension and had avoided feeding my hand into his amoeba-like paw a second time, and mine was pleasantly unsullied.

We chatted of movies, Grit and I.

Among his acquaintance his personal proclivities were notorious. When he visited a theater for his first viewing of Luchino Visconti's DEATH IN VENICE, he had stayed for a second viewing immediately. He had seen, when first released in theaters, Stanley Kubrick's BARRY LYNDON as many as 8 times.

Ingmar Bergman's CRIES AND WHISPERS he had seen perhaps a dozen times, revelling in the lush. John Ford's STAGECOACH he had seen scores of times: during one of his moodinesses he watched it every night for weeks, using it to begin each evening session he spent with himself.

What was he escaping? I wondered.

Can our ego escape its wounds? I wondered.

Whose decision is it? I wondered.

Grit explained upon provocation that he had turned for solace to movies, as to books, as to music. He did not explain his explanation, nor did I ask the pounding question.

Grit and I watched the superficial dishonorable bundle of clothing as it walked away from us, its duty assured. And we walked.

We dawdled outdoors in the queue, and we dawdled indoors in the lobby. We possessed similarly the unfortunate tendency always to be early, a tendency which could cause embarrassment under certain circumstances, and which did.

The pageantry of Goya's earlier century appeared and moved across the screen as if his portraits had been given legs and lungs which moved. As in his pictures the regal families resembled inbred appalachian moonshiners whose eyes were so alarmingly closely set that the right eyes were on the left, and the left eyes were on the right, nudging one another resentfully.

Goya was a man whose genius chanced.

As we walked pleasantly homeward Grit inquired what I chanced to be doing with my time, saying that it was necessary that a man always be doing something constructive, "Else why bother being alive?"

I told him, humbly, almost with my tail between my legs, that I was endeavoring to write a diary. I explained the difficulty of maintaining a rigid ingenuousness, while exploring ingenuities.

Having read a fair quantity of published diarists and diaries, he nodded knowingly, saying, "Honesty is an emblem of vitality, as is ingenuity. Also it's important to remain more the diarist than a diarrhist, if you'll forgive my reaching."

He meant it well, so I laughed.

And we saw the home-star gleaming in our window, welcoming.

Once we had entered our familiar atmosphere, I said, "Reciprocity is the fairest thing alive. You have asked me what I am doing in this portion of my living, so I reciprocate and ask you the same."

Just as you do when you enter your house and buzz about, we were only puttering casually, familiarly, easily. He looked over, not very absently, and said, "At the moment I am reading Edgar Allan Poe, in the newest collation by Thomas Ollive Mabbott. Tom collated every edition of Poe that was published during Eddie's lifetime,

and Tom demonstrates clearly just how intenser Eddie
was than was anybody else."

I said, "Is studying another man's psychological and
imaginative experiences quite the same as actually doing
something oneself?"

He said, "Especially if it's being done during an
interim, or in preparation for some other more personal
project. I have my eye on a story I wish to do, but my
mill needs grass and grist.

"And yes," he replied. "As I peeled back the west
Atlantic's germanic blackness of darkness it was
Hawthorne who caught my first eye, and Melville my
second, and now Tom has given me my third. Therefore
his work improves the species by elating me, and justifies
his strains.

"Every day I long for the evening," he said, which one
of my distant voices echoed cruelly, weighing it and
weighting it sadistically and masochistically. Healthier
voices shushed that distant voice ineffectually almost.

"Truth must have its day," he said, apropos of
something I supposed, I suppose. Jingo leaped and
attempted to turn himself inside out, then smiled and
yawned almost hugely enough to swallow his head.

Our little kitty watched from atop the curtain-rods,
having climbed the curtains. He smiled disdainfully,
almost, I thought. Kitties watch through walls, I know.

I said, "Admitting that each has been your favorite
among your many moments, and may be once again, or
twice or thrice again, describe them to me severally."

He said, "One cures topiaries in Eden's amber, and
one observes the generational mourning of expulsion,
punished as Job, endlessly possessing the wisdom of the
martyrs that no vindication is possible."

I said, "You missed one."

He said, "And one, himself his only metaphor, fascinated, looked into the sun's bright corridor where at the end a deeper fire raged. He was only a visitant."

I said, "Woof."

He said, "Heady stuff, indeed,"

I said, "The great study of Poe and Faulkner hasn't yet been written. Perhaps that awaits. Perhaps fate will fete you with that neat feat."

He said, "That would take Johnson and 40 years."

I said, "Woof."

He said, "Indeed. Yep."

The spider burst like a fuchsia pouched in his fingertips.

The evening had been cold, as cold, I supposed, as a winter's night in Covent Garden when all of the homeless people gather gregariously around the smudge-pots and roast potatoes, smoking cigarettes endlessly, and quaffing from little brown bags.

We had watched as the clouds gathered overhead, mantling the sky, and we could feel the temperatures rising. Everybody of every species slunk toward homes, we supposed.

In our home soon we separated, and I played in my room with our presumably lonely god, who greeted me from his perch on my curtain-rods as he surveyed his domain omnisciently, casting judgements in lieu of aspersions and incense.

The rains began, and soon the whole unholy storm broke, and shattered our living world. We understood we'd soon be without electrical power, since during storms it was commonplace. Grit and I each had batteried lanterns, used them.

I climbed under my pair of huge feather-filled blankets, mountains of downiness. How appropriate that we call them comforters, I mused.

God burrowed under the heap.

Rains and winds and lightnings and thundering lashed the house, spanking the roof and sides. I imagined a neglected coffee-mug overturned and spilling mildewed brew that was whitish with islands of life.

Animals were squealing.

I walked carefully into our livingroom and saw, as I expected, by my flashlight's beam, that Grit had left his door deliberately ajar. He snored softly as the down in my comforter.

Our livingroom window was open half a foot, as always.

I heard squealing on the porch, and I cautiously opened the door and a whimpering neighbor, small and wet and soaked with fright, scurried in and rushed trembling through Grit's doorway and into his bedroom.

This was Jingo's little skittish friend, who had ears longer than his tail, and a nose as wet as a fountain, and large dark luminous sad eyes hung like the storm lanterns of a ship.

My beam as I turned followed him through the doorway to Grit's bed, which was covered around its human form with a curling parade of cats. Every cat from our neighborhood, it appeared, had availed itself of the curious aura of protectiveness which my fatherly friend so naturally exuded.

The little dog and Jingo huddled restlessly on the rug, and I saw 2 other dogs beside them, like wagons in a circle, defending the thing that defended themselves. The brave cats did not stir from the blankets, except sometimes to extend a hand always to maintain contact if Grit shifted, and he was a shifter.

I returned into my bedroom, and found that god was on my bed, waiting. We huddled under blankets together, and somehow, certainly impossibly, were joined by another little kitty seeking salvation.

The night marched clangorously and settled toward morning.

Day began through my window.

I smelt coffee, wafting like forgiveness.

Grit was working patiently in the kitchen, his hand and its fingers scratching his belly-fur absently. He smiled pleasantly, said, "That was a hell regal of a night, little brother," and handed me a cuppa. The coffee was too hot yet.

Jingo frolicked, and greeted me jumping, swinging his ribcage at my legs, snuffling. I scratched his jowls and emitted appropriately foolish noises at him. His off-black eyes danced like the waters of hawaiian pools running with iridescent bulbous goldfish, and they danced now.

Our intruders had disappeared.

In my bedroom I discovered god alone.

As I opened the door the nonresident kitty slunk out, snuck once more to some unpleasanter reality. God remained a lump under the blankets, twitching and then not twitching.

That night the moon was no bloody galleon on a placid bay, nor was it a full-sailed bloody galleon almost on the rocks. The moon was a lady in her bath with her window closed, and though I tried to steal a peek I could not find her.

The world was grateful when a clearly hungover sun walked out the following morning and stood blinking. The air was clear. Except for our cat, god, and our 2 selves, the animals had departed our house.

Our phone rang, announcing the flooding of our lumberyard and our consequent temporary unemployment. To beguile the time and the times, idly I said, "What is the most beautiful word in our language?"

I had thought he might be stunned by the brainlessness of the question, but Grit only paused and replied, "Of course you have the question wrong. You mean to ask if I can spot that reticent recalcitrant, and if he stands alone, and if he exists only in our perceptions, and what defines the actual existence of beauty.

"James Joyce was asked, if only by himself, and he replied that the word was cuspidor. But if we read his books, we come away believing that his actual preference for the finest english was embodied in the expression: ineluctable modality. Which leads us mayhap to equate beauty with an exquisitely mouthed soundingness.

"Poe liked the expression, cellar door, which rhymes with cuspidor about as well as orange rhymes with door hinge.

"Having always been a preconceptual orphan, I prefer that devilishly friendly expression: residuary legatee. Notice how the tongue stabs exactly, delivering a sting Ariel would have approved."

My coffee clogged in my throat.

Grit said, "Precocious as you have become, you are too damn young to be drinking coffee, or anything stronger than mother's milk. It is only an administration of justice that you choke."

Both of us were laughing fit to die.

From the downy breast of the lioness feeds the lamb.

I can't quite remember if I've told you the name of this town we had settled in, but we called it Thrill Valley, or simply Thrilltown, and one evening I returned home from my customary wanderings, lured as I always was lured by the dim lamp we burned anytime either of us was away from our familial abode.

Grit was lying on his bed as I walked through the livingroom and peeked about, wearing only his socks and his flaringly loud boxers whiter than white roses and with luridly loud pairs of devils coupling on them in every conceivable friendly posture available to couplers. Our cat, god, was standing on his chest and they were rubbing noses delicately, doing what our socially insensitive forebears called eskimo kissing.

Grit was saying, "So, am informed you are a cat. How might you respond to such a libelous allegation? And what, I beg you to tell me, are your other and certainly far more mentionable accomplishments?" I didn't quite get the cat's answer, but then I did understand that when cats wish to speak exceedingly specifically to us as individuals talking to individuals, they can be adroit magicians indeed.

Had the answer been any of my business I am certain I'd have heard it quite clearly, as clearly as Grit heard it, I'm sure. My rested mind didn't bother to wonder if the red devils paused in their coupling endeavors to listen to the cat's response, and only a short while earlier in my life I would have wondered passingly, inarticulately.

Shushing our psychological extremities can be a significant accomplishment, I didn't bother to think. I asked Grit if he was planning to attend the town's annual parade on the following morning, knowing that if he attended we attended. Probably I had a preference but hadn't bothered to express that preference to myself, being aloof until called. Intelligently he answered, "Huh?"

And then he answered himself, "O yeah."

Thereby he informed me that he had been aloof as I, until called. I understood his tones as clearly as Jingo understood the meanings of our scents, as clearly as god understood the information in our fingers. Our gazes flicked across our fellow faces and we understood that, like Oblomov, we'd prefer to go.

On the following morning was scheduled the annual Memorial Day parade, a showcase for all of those various shenanigans one might expect to encounter in any small town's Memorial Day parade. The streets, we fully anticipated, would be stalled along the route, and cars would park in foolish places. Uniforms would be replaced by costumes, and by different uniforms. Some folks would hope, being eternally youthful, finally to be recognized for their heart's worth. And they would hope fervently that they might be permitted to recognize their recognizers.

Evil would still, apparently.

Frequently he and I complained privately that we were constitutionally unable to sleep even as late as into the sevens and the eights, and as was typical for us, though we were emancipated for the day and though we used no alarm clocks other than our internal clocks, we woke sometime in the excruciatingly early sixes, maybe about 6:11. We chatted and we whined, we fed and we puttered, we read the paper, and he disappeared again into his bedroom.

We were early so he returned into some book, Jonathan Edwards, I think, with his back on his bed and our cat on his chest, almost a meeting of the chins. I heard him saying affectionately, "Why do you have all the cutes? Didn't you leave any of the cutes for anybody else? How very very selfish is the kitty, to use all of the available cutes on himself...

"Surely you can recognize that that wasn't very sporting of you? By golly, I do suspect you might be a carnivore, albeit an endearing carnivore, yet a carnivore nonetheless..."

And so the amiable litany continued, until he had digested whatever knotty conundrum he had ingested, compliments of Jonathan Edwards. Being an impatient animal and enjoying my disgruntlement, I said clearly and yet quietly, with a faultless diction, "Wouldn't it be a trifle less masochistic simply to chaboogle over to the widow's boudoir and to cajole her into untying the too straight knot that is bent?" Certainly somehow in his capaciousness he heard me wholly and he scowled exasperatedly, and yet I was nothing if not an exasperating animal. Certainly I too had been conceived when lightning stung some leech-swum swamp, and I had been hatched when the moon too was a bloody egg.

I don't hesitate to admit that the parade was as

pleasantly boring as any old stick-in-the-mud might have wanted, and that, not being quite an old stick-in-the-mud, I had hoped surreptitiously that somebody would venture to misbehave. You know exactly what I mean. I didn't want for anybody to be hurt, but I wanted a lesser spectacle.

We watched the scouts, both girl and boy scouts, and various martial artists in groupings at various levels, and of course there was a generous complement of show-offs, local gentry, local politicians, fire trucks and police vehicles, motorcycles, people with tattooes and jewelries, people antsy for their daily drugs. Every racial tribe was represented, and every religious tribe that resided locally, and labor unions.

And there were girls flaunting their girlitudinous proclivities, with long skirts and with short skirts, with big blouses and with little blouses, with big hair and with little hair, tamed and wild, strung and unstrung, mad and sane.

And everybody behaved, even in the observing crowd. Even the attendant babies behaved, and the dogs. Grit commented, "The triumph of civility demonstates that honorable behavior needn't be foolish. People excel in the good and people excel in the bad, and we tend to praise the goodly excellent and to dismiss the badly excellent, though both exist equally and in a healthy atmosphere must be similarly acknowledged. That hairy jackass on the scooter, shooting in and out among the crowd, mildly endangering the feeble and the unwary, should be reprimanded constructively and if a nondemonstrative nonhumiliating criticism doesn't work he should be unilaterally bounced.

"That would be an honorable response to a behavior that is badly excellent," and his eyes and, I supposed, his mind turned to other matters, having expressed an issue.

I too had noticed the man on the scooter as he zipped recklessly, but I had preferred not to acknowledge his behavioral shortcomings. I watched as a man snatched his daughter from the scooter's probable path.

I glanced at Grit and he was attending something else.

I also noted that Grit was perhaps hairier than was the jackass on the scooter, but Grit was combed, civilly, and Grit lacked the other man's sheen of unwash. I thought, "Hrmph."

I thought, "Have we a snob on the premises?" But I am not certain that this latter speculation ever quite made it into actual words. Sometimes thoughts remained in that ineffable area of paradigms, just barely post-conceptual, certainly pre-natal. I wondered, and my wonderment did not become words, and I wondered about that.

Grit announced, "You create a monster when a man sees you endanger his daughter. Let's walk over by that jugband." I had thought, if I had thought about it, that his attention was miles away, but he had been feeling my speculations and my reactions. Perhaps he had been Holmesing my Watson again. I remember feeling disconcerted when I discovered that my most innermost stirrings were not only private. Initially it had seemed a betrayal, and then it had seemed an awakening, and ascendance.

When, I wondered, did things cease to shift?

And now I tried to understand how a jugband could play Gershwin and Stephen Foster. Goodness, goodness, goodness? Yes.

The singer looked like a cardboard angel, displaying lights that were not hers, and singing with a light she belonged to. Her voice was only a visitant.

I found a certain too participatory pleasure in watching the people too alertly. Always I began watching the carriages, the posture, and if I found the posture sufficiently intriguing, I would watch the face, and the neck and the hands, those wonderful human hands.

When we watch a human we discover the eyes fail at different speeds, and for different reasons. That man's right eye weakens earlier than does his left eye, because the eye in its interior is feebler although its exterior muscles might be stronger than are the muscles of the lefterly eye. Each eye in his face races toward closure, and the race has rules difficult to understand, difficult to locate, difficult to anticipate.

That woman's left hand enfeebles somewhat earlier than does her right hand, because of the supply of blood, because of its exposure to the sun and to the wind, because of its professional demands and because of its informal demands, because of the way she sleeps. Queerly although it may appear to our exploratory observation, her hands as she ages begin to appear cooked by the sun and by the winds of experience and of exposure, they mottle, they begin to burst preparatory to implosion, preparatory to an eventual collapse. They redden, and they empurple, and they blacken, because they are meat exposed, and her most intimate self is their burden.

I did watch.

Beauty is the spindrift and the waves that lap at the edge of absolute terror, of awe, and I could feel the beauty of the day in my stomach. Every place has its time and cannot be contemplated exclusively of time, and this land was a beautiful place, filled with redwoods in its valley, filled with people in its valley and in its hills, with coons and fish and birds aplenty. Wiser heads and wiser stomachs have pondered.

Can time be contemplated exclusively of place, I wondered, idlingly. And I wondered if the matters were confused by being accidental and therefore arbitrary. We are given ease by the absence of a whole encompassing matrix, I thought, though not quite in words.

Wiser heads and wiser stomachs have pondered, I thought.

Somewhere in this my passing expansiveness I glanced up at the controlled face of my friend, Grit, because I wished both to share the prospects of my temporary elevation, and because I wished to discover if he already through some manner of anticipation understood my experience. Grit had the disconcerting habit of prescience in everything concerning my existence, I believed, and when I looked into his facial configurations he smiled encompassingly, I thought, either because he anticipated my experience or because he was large enough to comprehend my smaller psyche anyway. Certainly I was reassured that my trial was appreciated, which is, after all, what we ask of deity also.

When those people with whom we live have the extended ability to provide this comfort it is a blessing, almost of a nonsecular kind. And I confess I was gratified, grateful, satisfied withal.

My experience turned outward once again, regaining my impersonal scrutiny of matters elsewhere. I watched an a cappella opera enacting in my midst, while I was in its midst. The whole involving world was midstful, enwrapping. God, I was blessed.

My knees didn't wobble visibly.

Grit said, "Let us ponder articulably the actual nature of appearances. What, precisely as we can express things, is demonstrated by this thing we call appearances? Appearances deceive only those beings who are unable to understand the function of appearances, as if they viewed things with an other light from an other source of light.

"Don't let's forget what a different appearance would be discovered by a whale or a dolphin, vastly intelligent beings in their other way who watch the way sounds bounce and home. And ponder the world Jingo sees, in which smells prefer a different function.

"We celebrate our eyes because we are dumb to the other sensings. Imagine the necessary confusion if our touch were expanded and refined, and we begin to crawl with terror.

"And now," he murmured, "let us ponder a salmon burrito, hot as Venus, bursting with beans and whole rice, cilantro aplenty."

"Indeed," I vowed.

Sometimes when the days and the evenings of the spring slide almost subliminally into the days and the evenings of the summer I could persuade myself that I loved those days and those evenings the most of all the days and the evenings of the rolling year, and I might not quite be lying.

On one early afternoon I sat watching television with the sound off while using its blue cyclopean light to read David's PSALMS. The program was in Mandarin and occasionally I glanced at it in an attempt to understand the people through an observation of their body language.

I heard a tapping on the screendoor, which bounced jerkily being tethered by its hook&eye. Being almost darkened in a corner and instantly realizing I was not the person sought, I stayed at my vigil, pretending ignorance and abstraction.

Grit moved in from the kitchen and approached the door, said hi to the postmaster's widow who was tapping lightly, swung the door wide after unlatching it, and stepped onto the porch. He understood exactly where I was, and probably understood my attitude exactly.

My attention of course tunneled through the intervening space and my ear found its niche between Grit and the widow, whose name was Dinah. She had, I thought, had a few drinks, and her loneliness had risen. She chatted at him and he chatted nimbly with her.

Of course I was a bit jealous, perhaps, although I knew of course I had no just claim to jealousy. I was angry because of it, and I gnawed my anger cleverly.

Grit stepped back into the room and latched the door as she stepped from the porch onto its first step at the top, and they looked at their opposable selves, each bemused. She stepped again toward the screen and pressed her breasts and her pelvis against the screen, flatly rotating her hands beside her hips grasping gently, never quite surrendering her essential balance.

Her lips pressed themselves gently but tightly against the screen, and he stepped forward again and with his fingertips he pressed against the screen against her pressing lips. He turned, turned again and smiled, and he returned across the carpet and through the door into the kitchen. She turned, catching perhaps a piece of my glance, and stepped off the porch and across our briefest of all possible lawns and she sauntered off.

I strolled immediately to the screen and watched her departure, her bottom undulating and rotating deliberately as if it were chewing and savoring an exquisitely delicious piece of warm soft caramel. I looked and located the merest hint of saliva where her lips had pressed the screen, and I touched my finger to it as Grit had done. I touched my fingertip to my lips and my tongue, watching her although she was gone.

I pondered grating a habanero against the screen, in just that very place, anticipating a recurrence. I pondered popping a zit exactly onto that spot. I swung about resigned, and touched the television into darkness.

Grit was an infamously rotten whistler. I suspect he filled his mouth with bits of broken cork preparatorily to the attempt, though typically I could discern which tune he strove to imitate. And now I heard him in the kitchen, while he puttered whistling the tune Dinah, and so I surmised that her visit at the least had not caused him to invert.

I said aloud though low, yet clearly, "I frustrate not merely because the little people are inevitably wrong, which they are not quite, perhaps, but because they are inevitably incomplete, and because my tongue has not the tactile clarity to inform them adequately.

"I lack the experience which might bring articulation, and yet I fear their perceptual hides are impenetrable to any articulation. It would be as if I spoke to a tree of the responsibilities of treeness, or if I explained to a bird the relative inferiority of wings to hands.

"And none can speak to me of what I need," I spoke toward and through the late noon-lit windows of the house. Trees and grasses were bending, and the winds were bending in the light which leaned against the earth so uncannily lightly. Gravity bent, and the magnets bent, and everything stood in a stoop.

Like a conductor whose face arrests the coiled ocean determining a huge migration of whales I raised my

arms and my hands in the darkness, and almost
undisturbing the silence wholly I spoke this the very
simplest of haikus:

Though the sun proceed
our names to carve in the sky
the sun's name too dies.

And I laughed without a sound.